Last Turn Home

a novel

Lara Alspaugh

This novel is a work of fiction. Names, places, and incidents either are the product of the authors imagination, or are used fictitiously. Any resemblance to actual persons, living or dead, events, or locations is entirely coincidental.

© 2018 Lara Aslpaugh
ISBN: 978-0-692-09085-5

Book design and editing by Poole Publishing Services LLC

For my E and our boys ~ Cooper, Jackson, and Aiden
Because of you

"Souls tend to go back to who feels like home."

— N.R. Hart

Chapter One

Marian Wallace was cutting vegetables for dinner when it happened. Above the sink, the arms of the clock pointed to 4:47 p.m. The table behind her was set: one blue placemat, one dinner plate, a single knife, fork and spoon. Sweat dripped down the outside of her water glass.

The pain had nagged her all day. It's true what they say, it feels like an elephant sitting on your chest. Deep pressure on her lungs crept like molten lava from her left arm to her jaw to her core. It was hard to breathe. She didn't clutch her chest like they do in the movies. Instead her breath became jagged and thin. Her body fell silently to the floor; first to her knees and then toward her side, her head sliding down and hitting the gray linoleum. The dry tip of her tongue escaped between the wrinkled lines of her faded blue lips. She blinked her eyes three times and closed them.

Marian Wallace was dead.

Chapter Two

Tessa looked at her reflection in the mirror. Her cheeks were flushed pink and her green eyes, highlighted with a honey halo around her pupils, danced. A thick halter strap gathered behind her neck and was anchored by a jeweled aquamarine diamond at the center of her chest; her satin gown was the color of melted milk chocolate. She swayed slowly back and forth in front of the mirror, watching as the gown hugged her hips, floating with liquid grace as it flared away from her knees. Her toes peeked out from under her gown. She was wearing a sexy strap sandal that Adrianna insisted was the only shoe acceptable to wear with this dress. Tess was capable of pulling together a beautiful ensemble on her own, but when A's Couture was giving her the dress for free, she followed directions.

"Adrianna, it's just gorgeous! Thank you so much!" Tessa gushed. She had been to a few extravagant events with Davis in the two years they had been dating, but this is the first time he invited her to his family's charity event for the Children's Action Organization. She wanted everything to be perfect. Tessa leaned toward the mirror, checking her makeup and reapplying her Pretty in Pink lip gloss.

"Stop touching my work!" Adrianna squealed. "You're going to mess up my lip liner." Tessa smiled as

Adrianna reached above her, tucking and spraying a few stray curls of Tessa's hair, colored a deeper shade than her natural basic brown at Adrianna's insistence. "It's what works with my dress," she had said. Adrianna stepped back to admire her handiwork. "Beautiful, dahling. Just beautiful!"

Adrianna was Tess's best friend in Chicago. Tessa Wallace has worked eighty to ninety hours a week at Chadwick, Holmes and Epstein as an associate attorney for three years, and her goal was to reach partner in seven more. It's ambitious, but that's Tess. It also means Tess didn't have much time for friendship. Luckily, Tess and Adrianna were grandfathered in long before the relentless hours. Broken plans and missed phone calls were the norm.

Adrianna and Tess met at the beginning of their sophomore year at Northwestern. Adrianna was an art major and Tess studied English. They became fast friends after meeting at a sorority rush party. Neither of them pledged Alpha Chi Omega, instead they became inseparable. Spring semester of the year they met, Adrianna transferred to The Illinois Institute of Art to pursue her love of fashion and design while Tess stayed at Northwestern to finish her undergraduate degree in preparation for law school. After Tessa finished law school and passed the bar, she began working at CH&E while Adrianna started her own fashion house in downtown Chicago, A's Couture. She had loaned Tess her dress for the evening in hopes of Tess being free advertising to the city's elite.

Adrianna was every bit the budding fashion designer: melodramatic, melancholy and magnificent. "The M-Trifecta of a successful designer," Tess told her. She loved to be the center of attention, which suited Tess perfectly as she preferred to be out of the spotlight. Tess was tailored suits and pencil skirts in varying shades of gray, while Adrianna was muumuu dresses, high waisted jeans and color. So much color. Davis couldn't understand their friendship, he found the M-Trifecta to be overbearing and plain dramatic (bordering on hysterical at times) — the polar opposite of his disciplined, refined girlfriend. He tolerated Adri for Tess.

"Oh my God, I forgot to tell you!" Adrianna shrieked. "I can't believe I forgot! I saw Mark at the Cheesecake Factory!"

"Ok wait, I don't know which is more shocking, the fact that you ran into Mark or that you were at the Cheesecake Factory…"

"Don't judge. I love their lemon meringue cheesecake. It's to die for. Have you ever had it? Oh I forgot you hate lemon, you really shouldn't hate lemon it's such a gorgeous flavor! I had a meeting with a fabric supplier that didn't go how I wanted. The cake helped. Well the cake and the lemon drop martini I had with it. I had a bit of a lemon craving going on."

"So…" Tessa prompted, "you saw Mark?" She leaned toward the mirror again, adjusting the edges of her eyeliner. Mark was Tess's college boyfriend. To be fair, they had technically been briefly engaged. They dated as college students do, frat parties and formals, late night movies and Tessa losing her virginity to a young and clumsy Mark without regret. Mark had graduated from Northwestern's business school and gone to work while Tess went on to law school. She graduated, passed the bar on her first try, landed her job at CH&E and he proposed. Their romance had never been particularly passionate or emotionally intimate, but Mark had been suitable, steady and he loved her. The problem was, Tessa loved her job more. Mark didn't want to live with a woman who did not, or could not, put her family first and Tess did not want to live with a man who could not support her superior drive. He had not been patient, and didn't wait for the demands of her work life to wane on her. Unfortunately for Mark, her determination for success only got more intense with time. After five years of dating, and only three months of being engaged, they parted ways. She had returned the half-carat diamond of dim light and color; she wished him well and didn't shed a tear. Adrianna had cried. She didn't have qualms about whose emotion she succumbed to; all life events were subject to Adri's overindulgence in the drama department. Tessa, however, couldn't bring herself to weep. Certainly she was fond of Mark and felt a measure of sadness, but largely what she felt was relief.

"Yes, I did see Mark. He was with his wife, Cindy. No, Katie. Chrissy? I don't know, I wasn't paying attention. Some basic, suburban woman. Brown hair with highlights, straightened like it's 1999 and she's Jennifer Aniston." Adri picked up the hot curling iron off of Tess's makeup table and began curling her auburn hair.

"And she was pregnant!"

"Really?" Not that a pregnancy surprised Tess. She knew Mark wanted a family, that was the last straw that broke their engagement. He wanted a baby sooner rather than later, and Tess... well Tess wasn't sure she ever wanted a baby. She was more surprised that someone her age would be a parent. She supposed it was about that time, but it wasn't on her radar. "Good for him! I am glad he got what he wanted."

"He's still cute as ever. I don't think Momma liked me too much. Or maybe it was just the big kiss I gave her Baby Daddy."

"Adri! Leave his poor wife alone. Poor girl, she doesn't know about the M-Trifecta that is A's Couture. You probably scared her to death. Not to mention, he is her husband now! And the father of her baby!" Tess chastised Adrianna, smirking as she spoke.

"I knew him first. Had to remind her of that. He was almost my best-friend-in-law, I guess." Adrianna cleared her throat and rimmed her own eyes with coal-colored waterliner, a skill Tess had yet to master. "He waited until she excused herself to go to the bathroom to ask how you were. Clearly, they have issues."

Tess's phone began to ring. "Can you see who that is? Make sure it's not Davis. Don't accidentally answer if it's my office! I'm not doing that right now."

"No name. 616-547-1863 Chapel Corners, Michigan?" Adrianna reported, turning to look at Tess. If she had been paying attention she would have seen the fear flicker through Tess's eyes before Tess was able to disguise it.

"It must be a robo call? Silence it, will you please? What are your plans tonight?" Tess diverted.

"Dinner with Armando!" Adrianna declared.

"Who the hell is Armando?" Tess asked as she collected her Pretty in Pink lip gloss, stole Arianna's lip liner pencil and compact mirror, and put everything in her jeweled purse for the evening. She picked up her phone, skimmed her thumb across the home button. The gray "New Voicemail" notification bubble floated across the picture of her and Davis in front of his parent's Christmas tree last December on her home screen. She slipped her phone into her purse, and turned her attention to Adrianna, who was waiting. "I'm listening!"

"He is gorgeous. He speaks very little English. I met him when I went out for drinks with Tamara and Molly last week. Remember? I told you!" Adrianna, unlike Tess, had a posse of friends. She had grown up in Forest Glen near Chicago. Her parents were wealthy (although Tess was never quite sure what they did) and Adrianna still kept in contact with a few of her high school girlfriends and hung out with several of the models she used regularly for her designs.

"I'm sorry, I forgot! I can't remember everything you say, especially when you are talking to me while I'm working," Tess pleaded.

"It's whatev. I know what my plans are this evening. What about you? Do you think tonight may be the night Davis finally pops the question?"

"Tonight? No, of course not. Tonight isn't really a

date, it's a charity thing." Tess busied herself with looking at her reflection in the mirror. Tonight would not be the night, Tessa was sure. The Children's Action Organization Gala was an important charity event for his family, Davis would never make it about himself. Tessa heard Davis let himself into her loft.

"I'm gonna scoot. Armando awaits! Have a lovely time — call me as soon as you can tomorrow I want to hear all about it!" Adri air kissed her work of art on each cheek, winked and went to greet Davis.

Tess could hear Davis and Adri chatting for a minute in the small foyer of Tess's apartment before Adri left. She gave one last check of her hair and makeup, a quick sweep with her eyes over her ensemble head to toe. Grabbing her clutch, she slid her phone out, looking one more time at the waiting voicemail before dropping her phone back inside her purse. The front door clicked closed behind Adri and Tess walked down the hallway to see Davis. She counted her foot falls, one-two, three-four, five-six, seven-eight, two beats for each step. The counting, which she did silently, helped ease her nervousness. She rounded the corner to see Davis looking out her window at her modest view. He turned to face her as he heard her approach.

"Wow. You look beautiful," Davis said.

"Thank you," she quietly replied. "You look awfully handsome yourself."

Chapter Three

Having the gala at Shedd Aquarium was Alma Renford's idea. She had wanted something special, something unique. This was it. Lights hung in delicate strands, dancing off the glass of windows and aquariums. The tables were covered in ocean blue fabric, delicate nameplates decorated with the tiniest of seashells marked each attendees place. Small bowls with Beta fish swimming with their tissue paper-thin fins centered the tables. Silent auction items were off to the right: Wrigley Box seats, a week's vacation in Cabo, a signed Patrick Kane Blackhawks jersey, among the treasures. An hour in and the gala was already a smashing success.

"Dad. Beautiful event as always," Davis said, stepping toward his dad in a warm handshake embrace.

"Glad you two could make it, Davis," Parker Renford said smiling at his only son. "Tessa, you look stunning." The older Renford took Tessa's hands in his and kissed her cheek. "Davis told me how busy you have been, thank you for making time to be with us tonight."

"I wouldn't have missed it." Tessa beamed. "I am so happy to be here, everything is so lovely." As much as Tessa cared for Davis, his father melted her heart. He had gifted his son his spirited blue eyes and dark hair (Parker's was admittedly more gray than black these days), and the years of his life wore well on his face. Although he was a shrewd businessman, he was never too busy or too important to be kind. Davis idolized his father, which was yet another reason Tess loved Davis.

"Where is Alma?" Tess asked as Davis handed her a glass of Dom Perignon off a passing waiter's tray, taking one for himself and handing one to his father as well.

"She was with me a few moments ago, I'm not sure who she got caught up talking to." Parker chuckled. "Please be sure to find her, she'll want to see you both." Parker and Davis's mother had been married for nearly forty years, and his face still lit up when he spoke of his wife. Tessa both envied and appreciated that. Davis and Tess hugged Parker one more time as he excused himself to work the room. Parker had been born into wealth and at times this embarrassed him. He was as well known for his philanthropy and generosity as he was for his business savvy. He and Alma started the Children's Action Organization twenty-five years ago as their personal way of giving back, and this evening was an important event for the Renford family.

"My dad adores you." Davis pulled Tessa close, hugging her gently.

"You think so?" The thought warmed Tess's heart. Tessa loved Davis for many reasons, his family and devotion to them was among the biggest.

"He isn't the only one, either." Davis kissed Tess's forehead, cupping the back of her neck with both hands. Tess closed her eyes and let his touch flood her with warmth. She tipped her head up and smiled. A moment of worry flashed across her eyes as quickly as a falling star. Before Davis registered what it was, it was gone. Tessa looked away and tucked her jeweled clutch under her right arm for safekeeping.

"Should we find our seats?" Tessa asked a bit too quickly. Davis nodded, feeling the energy between them change as sure as a cold draft through an old window.

. . . .

Davis tried to regain the promise of the night, something had happened and he wasn't sure what. Tessa was distracted. Davis squeezed her hand under the table, running his thumb across the back of her hand, smiling at her as she fiddled with the clasp on her purse. Was it Tess's imagination that he lingered over her ring finger, circling his thumb in the empty space? Tessa eyed her clutch again, and her heart jumped inside her chest and her hands became sweaty, knowing the message was lying in wait in her voicemail inbox gave Tess a shot of adrenaline-soaked anxiety.

Tessa and Davis had met because of her work at CH&E. Parker had gone to the University of Michigan with Robert Chadwick, a partner at Tess's firm, and therefore CH&E handled all of Renford Construction's legal needs. Tessa and Davis had met at a CH&E holiday party her first year with the firm, having both arrived at the bar to order a glass of champagne —their mutual drink of choice — at the same time. Having spent the evening chatting, weaving in and around each other at the party, Tess wasn't entirely surprised two weeks later when Davis sent two dozen red roses with an invitation for dinner at Giant in Logan Square. Tess initially declined, not interested in mixing business with pleasure, and she wasn't sure she appreciated the over the top gesture of twenty-four roses. She also thought maybe Davis was too good looking and perhaps even too extravagant to date. However, Davis persisted and eventually Tessa relented — his eyes were what finally got her.

While the first eighteen months of their relationship had been full of adventure and fun (they had surfed in Costa Rica, drank wine in Rome and sailed in Lake Michigan), the past six months had been different. In the beginning, the two rising stars agreed to put their careers before their personal life, fitting in time together when they were able and holding no ill will if the other was busy with work. Now, however, their time together held more weight. Their kisses lasted longer. Davis began rearranging commitments to suit Tess's schedule and she cancelled to squeeze in more time with him. He held her hand more often, texted her daily and they talked every night before bed. In the beginning, Tess had believed the affair would be short-lived, she hadn't thought she could hold Davis's attention for very long. She was wrong. Their unspoken agreement to enjoy each other while it lasted has given way to subtle hints of long-term plans and a future together.

Tonight Tess struggled to keep her mind focused on the conversation around the table. Davis carried the heavy weight of their end of the table talk, freeing Tess's mind to wander. She saw herself living in Davis's brownstone, she saw a ring, she saw a dress, she saw a future. She also saw the past. The two will not reconcile, she is sure. As if on cue the waiter arrived with the first course, a lovely salad with caramelized pecans, plump raspberries, and feta cheese nested in a bed of crisp greens. With every bite her distraction grew, the daydreams of her future bled into concern over the voicemail from her past hidden in her purse. She tried to focus on the conversation, to stay in the moment, to be mindful and present, but still the message lingered. The main course came and went with rave reviews: prime rib soaked in an orange-soy marinade, spinach and pine nut couscous as well as steamed asparagus and wonderful loaves of warm rosemary bread with sun dried tomato and basil dipping oil. Before dessert was served, Tessa excused herself to the restroom, squeezing Davis's shoulder on her retreat and clutching her purse to her chest as she walked away.

Taking her time, Tess wound her way through the maze of round tables and watery tanks, in no hurry to find the ladies' room. She turned to see Davis still following her with his eyes as she walked away. She smiled, casting her eyes downward, pretending to watch her step. There were parts of Tess that were so damaged she could not share them with anyone. Protecting those dark stories of her life had always been more important than holding dreams for her future — until now. She loved Davis in a way that she hadn't loved anyone before. For a year and a half Tessa had waited for Davis to walk out. She had waited for him to realize she was not who she seemed to be, to understand he was better than she deserved. But over the last six months Tessa had begun to believe that she could be enough. If she could shelter Davis from her past, if she could make him believe who she was now was all he needed to know, maybe they would have a shot.

Tonight she had watched him canvas the room, his kindness and gracious nature floated behind him like a river of goodwill and she was proud. Tonight, more than any night they had been together, he was hers. He loved her. She smiled and soaked up the joy of being Davis's partner, his girlfriend, his lover and his friend. She could have a future with him. Of course she could. She was safe with Davis, he had accepted her ambiguity about her past without pressuring her for more. He would afford her that privacy.

She clutched her small purse to her side, walking slowly as the gazes of the women and men she passed grazed her. Tess avoided eye contact that might draw someone into her space. She smiled, letting her eyes wander a touch above their heads, leading people to believe her painfully shy or, worse yet, rude and unapproachable. She was a mixture of ordinary beauty, respectful aloofness and warm sensuality; most women found her competitive and most men desired to be closer.

"Tessa!" Alma reached gently for Tess's elbow.

"Alma. It's so nice to see you! You look beautiful." The butterflies that migrated to her stomach when Alma was near swooped in with a flush of nervousness. Davis's mother was the definition of sophistication, class and kindness with just a touch of cool. As comfortable as Tessa was with Davis's father, she was equally as uncomfortable with his mother.

"Thank you, sweetheart. Is your dress one of Adrianna's?" Tess took a deep breath, the mention of Adrianna allowed the butterflies to quiet.

"It is. Adrianna let me borrow it. Isn't it beautiful?" Tess wanted to please Davis's mother. As kind as Alma was (and she was always gracious and kind), Tess could never gauge her warmth. Tess was uncomfortable in the company of other women, especially those she wished to impress. Her inability to connect with Alma was a vestige of her life without a mother.

"The dress is beautiful, but the model makes it stunning." Alma smiled broadly at Tess. Her son was smitten with this young woman. As soon as Davis was old enough to date seriously, she told him the One Rule of Dating she had for his choice in partner: whomever her son chose to spend his life with had to like Alma. Alma, for her end, promised never to give the young woman a reason not to like her future mother-in-law in return. Davis and Parker had laughed at the rule; they didn't understand.

Alma was wise, she was aware that she had lived a blessed life. Despite those blessings, she had known heartache. She knew love and women could be cruel. The rule was in place to protect Alma and Davis and the love they had for each other. If Alma didn't like his choice of wife, no one would ever know. If Davis's bride didn't like

Alma, everyone would know and Alma and Davis would suffer. Alma adored her son, she wanted him to have a life and family of his own. She was not a woman who interfered and hovered, she was not intrusive and didn't drop by unannounced. She didn't take care of his laundry or do his shopping. She had raised an independent, kind and honest man. She did, however, enjoy her son and wanted to keep the closeness they shared. She did not want to lose him to another woman completely, and her One Rule of Dating was meant to ensure she did not. She had seen her friends begin wars with their future daughter-in-laws over wedding details involving calla lilies and meat versus chicken. Invariably, their sons sided with their fiancées, fracturing their mother-son relationship deeply. Alma would not survive that. She would not argue over where they spent their holidays or what color the bridesmaid dresses should be. She would protect herself by being the perfect mother-in-law, she would give her future daughter-in-law a million reasons to love her and none to not. She knew her son well, and Tessa, if she would have him, was the chosen one.

"Oh my goodness, thank you." Tess's cheeks flushed and her eyes took a bashful glance down at the compliment. Tess held her clutch closer to her side. "Davis is at our table and I know he wants to see you. I was just headed to the ladies' room."

"I will go find him. I won't keep you, darling. Just wanted to say hello. Please come next Wednesday for dinner with Davis, will you?" Alma accentuated the invitation with a squeeze of Tess's arm.

Tess stuttered in her reply, "Oh... sure. I would love to, I'll ask Davis if he would like me to join you." Davis had a standing monthly dinner with his parents on the first Wednesday of the month. Tess had never been invited.

"I know he will. You two have a good night, please come find Parker and me to say goodbye before you leave." Alma kissed Tess on the cheek and released her arm as she turned to greet another guest on her way to see her son.

Tess ducked into a darkened hallway, searching for the restroom and a moment of quiet. The steel drum band that was playing in the main dining area faded and the click-tap, click-tap of her shoes began to resonate in her mind. *One-two, three-four, five-six...* Tessa replaced the rhythm of the music with the melody of her steps as she walked, counting quieted her mind. Her fingers toggled the clasp on her purse back and forth several times. Her cell phone taunted her, the red indicator light mocked her thoughts of a future. Spikes of anxiety stabbed her insides with fear. Down the hallway toward the ladies' room, purse in hand, quickened pace and quickened heart rate, she knew she wanted a future with Davis. She wanted this life. With Chapel Corners waiting in the wings to take it away, she had never been as sure as she was now.

The darkness of the hallway was softened by the gentle glow from a large tank to her left. She closed her eyes and took herself in her mind's eye to the lake, under the water, to the only place that had soothed her as a child. The memory surprised her, she hadn't thought about being in the water for years. She reached into her past to feel the cold water silky on her back, she sunk into the silence and returned to the place of peace she had found as a young girl. The memories soothed her. Breathing in and out, one big breath, she opened her eyes and reached her hands out to the wall, touching the cool glass under her fingertips. The tank was so enormous, that it seemed without boundary, giving the illusion that the creatures who lived there had the run of the sea instead of the confines of a measured life. A few clusters of rocks, a bit of vegetation and water — dark, silent water — filled the tank.

Tess had loved the water as a little girl, it was the silence she had been drawn to. She had never experienced buoyancy and privacy like she had when she was under the surf. The quietness of life could find you there, and she had desperately needed it in those early years. It had been more than a decade since she had swum in the lake, another casualty of leaving The Corners and all she knew behind. Slow to allow her eyes to focus on her faded reflection in the spotless glass, Tess gazed at the shape of her lips and her high cheekbones and petite nose. She could see her face was a little too long and narrow; still, tonight she felt beautiful. She steeled herself, pulled her phone out, and tapped on the voicemail icon. There, sitting in the box was the message. +1-616-547-1863 Chapel Corners, Michigan. Tess's finger hovered over the blue triangle that indicated "play" and instead quickly tapped "delete" and then "delete" again, permanently erasing it from her phone. Tess didn't know who the message came from, she only knew that she had no use for any message from Chapel Corners. Her quickened pulse began to slow. Just knowing the message was not harbored in her phone was enough to calm her down. She would protect her future by eliminating her past — again.

Her attention focused back on the tank in front of her just in time to see something swimming low to the rocks on the bottom of the tank. A shark's large body lunged from side to side. Tess fought her reflex to take a step back in fear. Touching the glass between them reminded her she was safe, she forced a look at the giant creature. Her back straightened into a rigid line, her eyes fixed on the shark as he moved through the tank. He continued to slink from side to side, darting first quickly and then moving slowly. Tess found her watered-down reflection tangled with the shark's profile. He swam in and around and through her, leaving her cold. Taking another deep breath, she rummaged the courage she needed to turn on her heel and walk back to the steel drums, back toward Davis, back where she was safe, counting every step that carried her away from the shark and Chapel Corners.

....

The key to Davis's brownstone stuck the slightest bit, causing them to giggle together. "Seriously?" Davis said, his breath catching. He smiled at Tess from the corner of his mouth; Tess had pulled his shirt up from under his belt and was running her fingers across his chest. Her back was against the door, playfully taunting him with kisses as he spent time wiggling the key in an attempt to let them inside. The door was cool on her back, as the air warmed by the May sun turned cooler under the moon's watch. The unseasonably warm day was giving way to a typical, early spring chill.

Tess reached her hands around his bare back, pulling her fingers down his skin slowly with an ache that vibrated between them. For Davis's part, he was still fumbling with the door in a sophomoric fashion that both intrigued and embarrassed him. What was it about this woman that had him in such a physical frenzy? He had dated women more beautiful, with more money and higher social standing; yet she held a mystery that had enthralled him from the beginning. Her silent confidence and hidden vulnerability was a cocktail that brought him to his knees. No woman had captivated his interest for any length of time, and he was both exhilarated and confused by his desire to both claim her and watch her run free. The door gave way under their combined pressure and they stumbled into the dark foyer of his brownstone, their feet beating their pulse on the ceramic tile floor.

He laughed as he scooped her up, one arm slung under her knees and the other cradled her shoulders, and kicked the door closed behind him; his fingers slid against the balmy, dark brown satin of her dress, deliciously aware of her damp skin. He had been waiting to have her alone since he had picked her for the gala, even offering to opt out of the evening if Tess had been game. She had made him wait. She had made him wait as every man in the room devoured her with their eyes. She had made him wait while those same men's wives were both cool and overly generous with their compliments of her. She had made him wait through dinner and the auction and the closing speeches by his father and mother. She had made him wait in the car on the way home while the driver had smirked at Davis when they climbed into the back seat. Could even *he* see that Davis was beside himself? Could he see that Davis was so overcome with desire for this woman that his thoughts were interrupted, making him both juvenile and egotistical with the knowledge that she would be coming home with him.

Now she looked him steadily in the eye, bringing his face toward her own. Her two feet planted firmly on the floor she kissed him with as much softness as he was consumed by urgency. She drew out the moment, holding his face in her hands, kissing him gently on his chin and neck. Tess was drowning in his longing and her own, trying to keep her heightened emotions in check. She was desperate to be close to him, to own him and feel safe, and this carefully choreographed act was designed and directed to do just that. Pulling her lips from his, she ran her fingers through his hair, stopping briefly to outline his strong eyebrows. The backside of her hand skimmed across his cheek, his face jagged with new growth, scratching her gently. Reveling in the moisture of their kiss lingering on her lips made her feel naked, as if Davis could see inside her gently offered heart. If he could see her ugly, scarred inside, he would walk out without a word. She fought off the fear of the past. She had overcome it all. She could be all that Davis wanted, she already was. Protecting it was key.

Davis could have seized this quiet moment and taken her back with his still intense passion, but he didn't. He waited. When Tess would not bring her eyes to his gaze he gently took his fingertips and found her round, soft chin. Tipping her head up toward his he pulled against her slightest resistance. "I've got you," was all he could think to say. Her commanding performance of control had been weakened by a magnificent display of vulnerability that matched his in every way. He was ready to go there with her, desperate even, to do so.

In the beginning it had been endearing; she was fully capable of unbridled passion that was followed by gentle embarrassment at the emotion they had shared. Now, Davis worried. He knew he was in too deep with Tessa to let her go. He knew if she left his heart would never recover. He also knew that she was scared, fragile, and not willing to let those cracks in her façade be exploited, even for a great love. It was not the physicality of sex — they had been compatible from the beginning. Tonight it was their intimacy that frightened her, and his vulnerability that concerned him.

Tonight, though, her pulsing body won out over her fear and she turned to Davis, eyes opened wide, free from tears, and she gave herself over to the moment. She set down her past, he let go of his illusion of control, they made their way to his master suite, their hands loosely held together by a promise of the moments to come.

Gently she pushed him down onto the bed. He was seated inches from her body, aching to touch her. She undressed carefully, letting her gown fall to the floor in a silky puddle. Slowly he reached for her.

Tessa's eyes locked with his for a moment, a flicker of connection that vibrated between the two of them, holding them in time, pressing them together. The energy from that spark traveled through their bodies, engaging them in a rhythm of love and passion that connected their souls to create a union they both longed for. Davis became translucent, his desire for her overtook all sensibilities he had managed to carry with him to this point and he made love to her with fierce, magnetizing devotion. Never had she come to this place with a man before. Never had a man come so close to her heart, seen thru her the way Davis did. He knew she had secrets. Yet, he didn't care. He pulled her close, he nudged her toward him, he was patient and kind and waited and tonight she had given in. It was humbling to be so broken, to begin life with nearly nothing and to find the strength to rebuild yourself in a likeness you can be proud of, brick by brick. Tonight, Tess reveled in the humility. She was blessed by her past and buoyed toward her future.

By morning, the sun peeked gently into Davis's room, spilling warmth onto the bed and waking Davis from a sound, satiated sleep. His eyes were slow to open, but the smile that spread across his lips told the story of the night before. They had done it; they had finally bridged the gap that held them at such distance. He was certain of their future, certain of his love for her. Sliding his hand under the sheets searching for her warmth, his hand stopped. The sheets were cold and damp. Tessa was gone.

Chapter Four

Davis wasn't accustomed to drinking on Sundays. Regardless, the Vanilla Java Porter was cold, hearty and settled into the spaces where he was angry. He punched the pool stick toward the eight and watched the ball skim the corner pocket. "Shit," he said.

Ryan, his cousin and best friend, lined up the eight ball, and sunk it into the far corner. "Thank you very much." He smirked as he took the fifty-dollar bill Davis had slapped on the edge of the table. The two were born six weeks apart to the elder Renford brothers, and both worked at Renford Construction. Davis was on the business end, while Ryan was a project manager. He wore Carharts and steel toe boots to Davis's suits and ties. Neither man had any siblings, but they were as close as some brothers ever hoped to be.

"Asshole," Davis answered as he tossed his stick back into the pile and sat down at the bar, drawing his attention to the baseball game on ESPN. The Cubs were two games down in the first series against the Cardinals. Kris Bryant sailed one into center to tie them at 3-3 in the bottom of seven in game three. "That dude is ridiculous."

"He is a beast." Ryan slung himself on a stool next to Davis, turning his attention from their pool game to the now interesting Cubbies play.

"Two more, boys?" Gretchen, their usual waitress at Shorty's, cleared their empty pint glasses and wiped down the space on the bar in front of them.

"I'm going to switch it up. Can I get a Goose and soda with a splash of lime, please?" Davis asked.

"Sure thing! What about you, Ryan?"

"Following his lead. I'll take one, too." Ryan answered. He looked toward Davis, who was staring intently at a Lexus car commercial. "So, are you going to tell me why we're here?"

"What are you talking about?"

"Dude, I don't think you have ever called me on a Sunday afternoon to play pool and drink."

"Nothing's up. I just wanted to watch the Cubbies, get a beer."

"And that beer just turned into vodka. You are the most disciplined guy I know. You don't drink on Sundays. You run, organize your shoes, iron your shirts, read the paper — you do Davis shit. You don't drink on Sundays. Sunday Day Loads are not your thing."

"You make me sound like a boring old fuck." Davis laughed.

"You said it, not me. Are we going to sit here and drink until you are so drunk you forgot why you called me?"

"Maybe."

"Your call, dude. Ready to hear it when you are ready to spill it." Gretchen set a fresh vodka soda in front of each of them, smiling in Davis's direction and glancing toward Ryan. Gretchen knew that Davis and Tess were together, but this Sunday she was taking the opportunity of a missing Tess to remind Davis she was interested.

"I don't get it," Davis said, staring now at Anthony Rizzo taking practice swings during a pitching change.

"Don't get what?"

"Tess. I don't get her at all."

"Ahh, trouble in paradise?" Ryan stirred his drink, punching at the lime with his straw. Ryan had been happily married to his high school sweetheart, Jamie, for five years. They had two kids, a son Matty who was four and a daughter, Gracie who was two. Ryan's wife was a soft, blonde, stay-at-home mom who baked chocolate chip cookies and packed Ryan's lunch every day.

"That's just it. We are perfect on paper. We should be in paradise. She's smart, sweet, funny. She's a worker, nobody works harder. We have a lot of fun, we have put in the time. She's always up for an adventure. But, it just seems like we are never going to make it happen." Davis paused, fiddling with his straw, chewing on the end. "I love her. I do. But I don't know if I can live with the constant distance. She won't let me in. Not all the way, anyway." Davis toyed with telling Ryan about their night together, how intense it was, but that wasn't really what this was about. This wasn't about her leaving. It was about why she left. And why she left without a word.

"She's a good girl, for sure," Ryan agreed, still stabbing at his lime with his straw, leaving space for Davis to continue.

"You know I've never met her family. Nobody. Two years, dude. We have been together for two years. The only person from her life that I have met is her best friend from college, Adrianna — who I can't stand by the way — and her assistant Lucy. I don't even think she has any family — how stupid is that? I've been dating her for two years and not only do I not know any of her family, I don't know if she has any family! What the hell?" Davis took a long swig of his drink, tapped the glass on the bar signaling to Gretchen for another. "It just seems harder than it has to be. That's all. And I don't know if it's time to cut bait or if I should stick it out a little longer."

"I can't tell you if it's too hard, you gotta figure that out yourself. The only thing I can say is that it's hard sometimes, no matter who you love. I love my wife, she's my best friend, she's awesome. But sometimes, it's just hard. And actually, it's harder more often than I thought it would be. It's harder than it looks from the outside."

Gretchen interrupted, "Do you guys want to order any food?"

"Yeah, probably should. I better eat, Jamie isn't going to want to feed me when I get home after I left her alone with the kids all day pouring on a Day Load with you."

"Sorry, Ry," Davis smirked.

"Don't be sorry. It'll just be one of those nights that are harder than others," Ryan quipped. The cousins sat together watching the Cubbies and then the Yankees, eating burgers and fries and adding a few more vodka sodas to their total. The duo did not discuss Tess again. Instead they discussed work, Ryan's kids and baseball. There was always baseball; they had both been solid players in high school, Ryan had a scholarship to play in college but tore his labrum and ended his career. When the check came, Davis grabbed the bill. "Least I can do is pay the tab since I put you in the dog house."

"Yeah, no shit you are paying the bill." Ryan laughed as Davis pulled his wallet out, slapped down his Am Ex and thanked Ryan for coming to his rescue. "No worries, cuz. I'm always here for you, you know that."

Davis grabbed the receipt, joking he was going to turn it in as an expense since they did spend a fair amount of time discussing the Darling project. He looked down at the receipt and noticed Gretchen had left him her phone number with a heart under her name. Surprised, and fueled by too much vodka, Davis looked up and caught her eye. She smiled again, "You guys have a great night, be safe!" Her blonde curly hair bounced as she worked behind the bar. She couldn't be more than twenty-two years old.

"You too, Gretch. See you next time." Maybe it didn't have to be hard. Maybe it could be as easy as Gretchen, the cute, blonde bartender. Davis tucked the receipt, and Gretchen's number, inside his wallet and headed home.

Chapter Five

Click-tap, Click-tap, Click-tap, seven-teen… eight-teen… nine-teen… twent-y. Tess counted the rhythm of her shoes down the grand tile hallway of Chadwick, Holmes & Epstein. Starbucks tall skinny chai latte in one hand and a light blue, tailored raincoat draped over the other, she counted the last nine steps to her office door. She breezed a good morning to Lucy, and saddled the door open with her right hip. Reaching over to flip the switch for the overhead lights, her tea escaped the cup and drizzled down her arm under the cuff of her starched white blouse. "Dammit!" she whispered, "dammit, dammit, dammit!"

"Everything okay, Tessa?" Lucy asked.

"Yes, I'm fine, Lucy. I just spilled my tea… again."

"I'll get you some paper towels." Lucy had followed her through the door into her office, propping the door open the rest of the way.

"No need, I have some in here from the last time." Tess smiled as she expertly slid the corner of a paper towel under her cuff soaking up most of the sticky tea before it came in contact with her blouse and licked what had dripped onto her palm. "I have to check my messages and then could you check on the updated Hartford file. Drew was supposed to have it ready on

Friday afternoon for me to work on over the weekend. I called his cell three times on Saturday with no answer."

"He dropped it off this morning, it's on your desk." Lucy smirked with her voice as she and Tess shared an exasperated roll of the eyes. Drew was famous for good work — good, late work. He obviously thought Monday morning was equivalent to Friday night.

Lucy had been her executive assistant since Tess started with CH&E three years ago. She was excellent: efficient, quick-witted, and a bulldog on the phone. She was also non-obtrusive into Tessa's personal life, and kept hers to herself as well. Lucy was ten years older than Tessa and about forty pounds heavier. Tessa did know she was a widowed single mother of one daughter named Emma, and that she had been dating again. She only discovered that because Lucy had received a dozen roses a few weeks ago, which happened to coincide with a dreamy smile floating on Lucy's face. Tess thought fondly of Lucy, even worried about her and Emma, but she could never nurture those feelings into an outward overture of friendship.

"Great, thanks. I guess my voicemails lit a fire!" Tess smiled. "I'll be here for the morning and then I have the meeting with Holmes this afternoon."

"I printed everything you sent over last night. It is all ready for you. Let me know if you think of anything else. I'm sure you are completely prepared." Lucy walked out the door with a kind smile and a flip of her full-figured red hair.

Tess's office was the color of peanut butter with

carpet that matched. She had built-in mahogany cabinets lining one wall, while the opposing wall was glass from floor to ceiling. The CH&E building was octagonal in shape with a grand water feature directly in the center. Stan Epstein had convinced Chadwick and Holmes that legal matters were stressful and he had learned that water had a calming effect. He theorized that there would be less anxiety, aggression and conflict involving clients and staff if they could reap the benefits of water therapy while in the office. He was also the man who had hired a yoga instructor for the staff members that met in the main conference room five mornings a week.

Tess received seven voicemails and thirty-two emails since she had cleaned out her inbox last night at home. She fidgeted in her ergonomically-correct chair and pulled at her black pinstriped pencil skirt. She was sorting through her emails while mentally preparing a list for the day when Lucy beeped in. "It's Adrianna from A's Couture on the line for you, Tess."

Hearing the smile in Lucy's voice she stifled a laugh. "Thank you, Lucy." Adri had insisted upon referring to herself as "Adrianna, from A's Couture" ever since she had opened her boutique fashion house four years earlier.

"My pleasure," Lucy said.

"Adrianna, this is Ms. Wallace from Chadwick, Holmes & Epstein. How can I—"

"She does not like me!" Adrianna wailed.

"Who?"

"What do you mean 'who'? Lucy, that's who. She acts as if we've never, ever met!" Adrianna verbally flipped her hair across her shoulders and onto her back.

"*You* act as if you've never met. Besides, Lucy likes everybody."

"Except me. I don't know what I ever did to her. I'm always polite, I always—"

"Can I help you with something this morning Adrianna from A's Couture? Or did you just call to whine?"

"I am not whining! I am simply stating that your secretary—"

"Adri, it's me. You're whining. Stop it. And she's my executive assistant, not my secretary. I'm busy, I have a huge meeting with Holmes this afternoon. What do you need?" Having forgotten that she had not spoken to Adrianna since the benefit on Saturday night she was pleasantly agitated with her best friend.

"What do I need? I need you to remember that I have been on pins and needles here—"

"I'm sorry! I'm so sorry. I forgot to call yesterday. I was so tired from work all day on Saturday and the benefit went late and..." *Davis*. Her voice faltered and as her words faded Tessa realized, and not for the first time, one of the benefits of having a self-absorbed best friend was that when Adrianna was on a jag she was oblivious to anything but meeting her immediate needs. Tess had been replaying Saturday night in her mind since she left Davis's brownstone, her stomach twisting into knots every time she thought about slipping out from under the covers while the man she loved slept.

"Darlin', I couldn't care less about the benefit. What

did people say about my dress, and did you tell them you got it from me?" Adrianna was truly an artist, and her medium was fashion. She invested herself into every design she produced and thus was equally invested in the response. Plus, she loved attention. If she could, she would have sewn her A's Couture label on the outside of the gown rather than the inside.

"They loved it."

"What does that mean, 'they loved it'? That doesn't mean anything! Give me words, I need adjectives, I need feedback. I need—"

"Exquisite. Delicate. Delicious. Enchanting."

"Yeah, what else? Who said delicious?"

"Davis."

"He does not count, you know that! Who said enchanting?"

"Meredith Bancroft."

"Eww, you talked to the Bancrofts?" If there was one thing that Adrianna of A's Couture knows, it is the dark side of Chicago's upper crust. She grew up in Chicago as a trust fund baby raised by a succession of nannies. Evidently it had been difficult to retain an au pair who would deal with Adrianna's dramatic flair. That kind of upbringing provides you with a certain education; Adrianna's own grandfather had spent seven years in prison for tax evasion.

"Yes, and it was lovely."

"You liar. That woman is hardly tolerable sober." Tess laughed in an attempt to disguise the clicks of her keyboard as she typed out an email.

"Are you doing your email?"

"I am at work."

"You can't give me five minutes? I think Robert Holmes can spare his star legal slave for five minutes! Stop typing, Tess! I mean it."

"Okay. I'm not typing."

"You're reading. I can tell. I can tell when you're not listening to me."

"Okay, not typing, not reading. Is there something you need?"

"No, not really." Adrianna paused, "My mother is having a luncheon next Sunday and you have to come with me." Her words came out in rapid fire, despite her attempt to draw them out as much as she could without being accused of whining again. Tess could hear Adrianna holding her breath.

"Sunday? Yeah, I don't think I can. I'm busy. I'm sure I'm busy. I'm so sure that I don't even need to check my calendar." Adrianna and her socialite mother, Linda O'Leary, were competitive about everything: weight, age, career and attention from Frank, Adri's father. They behaved more like siblings than a mother-daughter duo. In college Tess had spent holidays and weekends with the O'Learys. She had traveled the world, tagging along on their family vacations: skiing in Vail over Christmas, Mexico for spring break and once out east to Rhode Island to whale watch for Mrs. O'Leary's (fifth) fiftieth birthday. Tess was grateful for all Adrianna's family had done for her, it was Mrs. O'Leary's suggestion and help that earned Tess the scholarship from CAO. Tess would have spent many Christmases alone if it wasn't for their open arms. Still, they were exhausting.

"Tessa Wallace. You are my best friend and with that title comes responsibility! And besides, I need you. And I gave you the dress! Come on, please, please, please, please—"

"You're whining. Why do you need me?"

"Puhleeze!"

"You're going to call me all day until I say yes, aren't you?"

"Absolutely."

"Yes, I guess I should be able to leave work for a couple hours," Tessa conceded. "You still didn't answer me, though. Why do you need me? What's up?"

"Thank you, so much. I am forever in your debt!" Adrianna sounded contrite enough that Tess smiled. "No reason in particular, Linda is just driving me cray cray lately. Literally. She's so dramatic it's ridiculous." *Pot. Kettle.* Tessa thought. "She's so much calmer with you around, *you're* the daughter she always wanted, you know."

"I am far too plain to be Linda O'Leary's daughter and you know it. She got exactly what she wanted: a diva, prima donna pain in the ass," Tessa quipped. "Listen, I have to go, you're not exactly a billable hour."

"Nice. Thanks. I do, too. I'm expecting a fabric shipment any minute and the last time those bastards left three bolts of Italian silk outside in the rain. I mean, who does that? I obviously can't trust—"

"Goodbye, Adrianna." Tess clicked the phone back

into its receiver and focused on her computer screen.

....

The morning passed in a mountain of paperwork that simply divided itself into smaller mountains of paperwork. Just before noon, Tess stopped to order a chef salad from the deli across the street from CH&E. Her mind had been solidly on work, but she could still feel Davis simmering on the back burner of her mind. His chest rising and falling as he slept, his eyes closed as he moved on top of her, his warmth as he cradled her to sleep. *Why hadn't he checked in with her? Was it that unreasonable to leave? Why did she leave anyway? Not even a text?* She glanced at her phone tucked in the top drawer of her desk. No notifications. Nothing new. She longed to reach out and touch him, to hear his voice to see his name on her phone, yet she couldn't seem to bridge the gap herself.

Lucy rang when her salad was delivered and she realized that she was starving. While she ate Tessa scanned a new list of emails, answering those that required immediate attention and making notes on what needed to be done to complete the train of work begun by the others. There were three forwards from Adrianna, exactly two friendship chains and one letter claiming money would rain from the sky via Bill Gates for every email that was sent through the ultimate email-tracking device. Tess smiled at her friend and deleted times three. *How does she get any work done?* Tess wondered with a smirk.

At first, Tess ignored the ringing phone. Lucy typically answered her line in two rings, max. When the phone continued to ring, Tess peeked out the window in her door to see that Lucy had stepped away from her desk.

"Chadwick, Holmes & Epstein Law Offices, this is Tessa Wallace, may I help you?"

"This is Tessa Wallace?"

"Yes, this is Tessa Wallace, may I help you?"

"Um… yes, this is Mr. Lanford, Mr. Roger Lanford from Lanford and Associates in Chapel Corners, Michigan."

Tess froze. She cleared her throat before answering. "Yes, Mr. Lanford, what can I do for you?"

"I'm terribly sorry for the nature of the call, Ms. Wallace. Your grandmother, Marian Wallace, passed away last Tuesday."

"Oh… um… thank you for calling, Mr…. um…" Tess brought her left hand to her forehead in an attempt to steady her shaking. Tessa felt a wave of nausea. This was the message she deleted on her cell phone!

"Ms. Wallace, are you okay? Is there someone with whom—"

"I'm fine, Mr. Lanford. Thank you for calling. I really need… I really need to get back to work—"

"Before you go, Tessa… may I call you Tessa?" Mr. Lanford continued without waiting for a response, "I am your grandmother's attorney. She has named you as her executor. There are not substantial assets, but there is something at stake. I was wonder—"

"I don't want any of her money. None of it. I don't want anything. Thank you again for calling, Mr. Lanford, but I really do need to go."

"Ms. Wallace, the house that you grew up in—"

"I said I don't want anything from her." Tess answered Mr. Lanford more forcefully than she intended. Her hands were slick with sweat. She wanted to slam down the phone, but she didn't. Visions of her grandpa Henry's den flashed in her memory, a vintage slide show in her mind.

"I understand you are feeling very strongly about this right now and perhaps we can discuss it at a later date. Being a lawyer yourself you must understand that you are the appointed executer of your grandmother's will and that does entail certain responsibilities. The house will need to be put on the market, after it is cleaned out of course."

"Cleaned out! You think I am going to come up there and clean out that place out?" Taking a deep breath and closing her eyes, Tessa stood from her desk. "Look, Mr. Lanford, I have not spoken to my grandmother… to Marian Wallace, for eleven years. I do appreciate you calling and telling me of her passing, but as for being the executor of her estate you must be mistaken. The woman hated me, there is no way she would have willed her house or any other asset to me."

"Ms. Wallace, I am aware that you have had a strained relationship…"

"Strained would have been doable, Mr. Wallace." Now standing at her desk, Tess left her insecurities behind and worked into full-on lawyer mode, handling Mr. Lanford as she would her client's opposition.

"Tessa, I am not mistaken. Your grandmother made you the executor of her will some time ago, when you turned twenty-one. I can send you a renunciation if you aren't willing, but perhaps you should take some time and think—"

"I don't need any time, I don't want her money. I don't want anything to do with her."

"Fair enough, I understand. The renunciation form will need to be signed and filed."

"I'm sorry, Mr. Lanford, I have a call coming in that I have been waiting for all day. I will get back with you. Thank you again." Not giving Mr. Lanford another moment to respond, Tessa replaced the phone receiver in the cradle just as her knees fell under the weight of the past and she collapsed in her chair. "This is not happening. I will not go back there. I am not doing this again. There's no way. She's probably not even really dead. She probably made this crap up just to watch me squirm, turn me into a mess." *No way. Absolutely not.*

"Hey, Tessa." Lucy poked her head around the doorway. "I just got back to my desk and I could kind of hear you... are you okay?"

"Lucy, hey... um... I forgot you were out there. I, um... just got some news..." Tessa absently straightened and sorted the piles on her desk as she spoke.

"Tessa, what's wrong?"

"Nothing. Nothing's really wrong." Tessa reached up and pulled her hair reflexively into a ponytail. "You know what? I have to go." Tessa walked from around her desk, stumbling slightly as she reached the corner. She grabbed her purse from the chair and slinging her rain coat over her shoulder on the way out the door. "I have a... um... I have a family emergency. Will you call Holmes for me? Drew can pick up where I left off on the Hartford case, I'll be gone for a couple of days."

"Tessa, hey, what's the matter? What's wrong?" Lucy's face showed the concern of a friend and Tessa fended it off efficiently.

"I'm fine, Lucy. I'm fine. I just have a few things... a few things to take care of. I'll call tomorrow and check in. I'm sure I will be back Wednesday morning." With that Tessa breezed past Lucy without so much as a backward glance. Click-tap, click-tap, click-tap... *one, two, three, four...* she counted her steps until she reached her car.

....

Davis didn't go into the office on Monday. He had woken up with a hangover, from the booze and from the lack of sleep. He had spent the night tossing and turning, dreaming. He dreamt of Tess and Gretchen. He dreamt he was playing third base for the Cubbies. He had a text waiting for him in the morning.

RYAN: Got a little spark knock this morning? My effing head hurts!

DAVIS: Yeah. This is why I don't do Sunday Day Loads. Working from home today.

RYAN: Sunday Day Load. Monday playing hooky. WTF are you going to do Tuesday? Will the Real Davis Renford please stand up… please stand up

DAVIS: Fuck Offfff

Davis laughed and threw his phone on his desk. He had thought a lot about how Ryan had said it's always hard sometimes. He had thought about Gretchen. It would have been easy to call her last night, he was drunk. Hurt. But the Real Davis Renford had stood up, been disciplined, and left the receipt with her number tucked in his wallet. He wondered why he hadn't thrown it away. He hadn't texted or called Tess either. He didn't have an answer for either action.

He didn't want to call Gretchen. He wanted to call Tessa.

He wanted Tessa to let him in, to want him as much as he wanted her. He wanted Saturday night to be where they moved forward, he didn't want it to be where they ended. He also knew that what he wanted wasn't necessarily what he was going to get. As much as he hated to admit that he didn't want to live without her, it was evident in every corner of his life. He was in love with Tessa Wallace. Deciding if he could live without her was now the question on the table.

There were so many subtle hints that Tess was hiding something, afraid to give him too much. He knew her parents were dead, he knew she had no siblings and she left her hometown right after high school graduation and hadn't been back. She had been to his parent's home, met

his aunts and uncles, shared their ho]
seen his baby pictures. He didn't ever
the town she grew up in. His anger
pull from the moon; he had given her
and he had been willing to take so little in re
Simultaneously angry and desperate, Davis was not in a
comfortable place.

He had managed to get a few hours of work done,
throwing himself into the minutia of email and
spreadsheets and quoting. Soaking his brain in numbers
and putting out fires gave him a welcome respite from his
repetitive thoughts. Around lunch he pulled on his Asics
and grabbed his headphones. A quick run and he would
be back at his desk. He scrolled through his playlist and
settled on The Marshall Mathers LP, thanks to Ryan. As
Eminem filled his ears, he relaxed into the rhythm of a
quick-paced mile.

Tessa was different. She wasn't interested in his
money, or his status. If anything, those things
disinterested her. She had not given in to his first request
for a date. Ryan had teased him that he pursued her
because he couldn't stand the fact that she rejected him to
begin with. Davis laughed, a nod to his competitive
nature, but he knew. He knew it wasn't winning he had
wanted, it was Tessa. She had a sadness in her soul, it
flashed across her eyes like headlights on a dark road at
night and then disappeared. It was this sorrow behind her
eyes he was interested in. At first he had wanted to save
her from it; now, he wanted to understand it. He wanted
to know her, wanted her to share that sadness, let him

a small part of it.

He rounded the corner of his neighborhood and neaded toward Grant Park. He had intended to head out for a short run, but his legs were strong and his lungs were craving more. His feet pounded the ground with more intensity than was needed, and his pace got quicker as the miles got longer. He reached the lake and slowed his steps. All his life he had lived next to Lake Michigan, its presence commonplace despite its magnitude and power. Davis lifted his arms on top of his head, wiped sweat away from his eyes and took a deep breath. The sun was warm on his shoulders. A taste of summer had swept into Chi Town weeks earlier than usual. Davis knew it would be short-lived and that the cold arms of Old Man Winter hadn't had their last punch, but he enjoyed it for the moment.

Running had given him the clarity he needed. Drinking with Ryan yesterday was helpful, but really it was Gretchen that had made up his mind. She had been tempting, and the fact was he still hadn't thrown away her number — but she wasn't real. Tess was real, Tess was where his heart was. Standing on the edge of the great lake, Davis was grounded, grounded in a way he hadn't been in months. The water stretched on, seamlessly meeting the horizon. It made him feel small and somehow made Tess feel closer. He turned on his heel, picked up his pace, letting the tightness of stopping to look at the lake work away from his bones. After all his indecision, he was headed home to call Tess.

Chapter Six

It was her earliest memory. She didn't remember much specifically, there was more recollection of her feelings than of the details. She had been sitting on his lap, she was maybe four? Five? He always began the stories by whispering in her ear, the exact words she could not recall, but she remembered their gentle intent and she always knew why the words were uttered in a whisper. Marian was not to know of their conversation. "You are not alone, my Tessa. You will never be alone. Your momma is always with you."

The picture he gave her to hold while he regaled her with her momma's adventures burned brightly in her memory. She was never sure if the minutia of the photo in her memory was accurate (Was her shirt pink, or red? Her shorts denim or white?) but that had never mattered. Those secret moments when Marian was out, when Henry would pull Tessa up on his lap and tell her stories of his daughter, her mother — their Caroline — that Tessa kept in a pocket deep in her soul were a soothing balm on a young spirit so bruised. She held Henry's stories in a place where reality dimmed and the life she pined for came to life. A place where her mother, always a teenager, forever a hippy, never left her, where Marian was absent and where Grandpa Henry lived forever.

She heard of her mother's adventures, of winning swim meets, of hiking the Sleeping Bear Dunes — racing all the way to the bottom once the climb was complete! She listened as Grandpa Henry told her about Caroline's first trip on the ferry across the Straits of Mackinac to Mackinac Island and how Caroline got to sit in the captain's chair and steer the boat. Caroline and Henry's adventures were many, and Tessa loved to sit upon her grandpa's lap and hear them all.

By far her favorite was the story she called "Tall Trees." She had heard it so many times, Tess could hear Henry from memory. Henry, Marian and Caroline were traveling to visit the nation's capital. All the way to Washington D.C.! The trip was long and Caroline couldn't wait to see all the monuments she had read about in school. Her favorite was the Lincoln Memorial. Henry would use his hands as he spoke, talking of the drive through Virginia, showing Tess how tall the mountains were, how vast the vista seemed as they drove through the Shenandoah Mountains. An eight-year-old Caroline became fascinated with the trees, proclaiming loudly, "Those are the tallest trees I have ever, ever seen! They must be one hundred million feet tall!" Henry always stopped to chuckle at this point of the story, so tickled he was by remembering his young daughter's view on life.

"I don't suppose those trees are any taller than some of the ones we have at home," he offered Caroline.

"Yes they are, Daddy!" Caroline insisted. "Look! They almost reach the sky!" It was then that Henry would tell young Tessa he realized that Caroline didn't understand the mountains. She thought the trees grew taller in Virginia, it hadn't occurred to her that the ground swelled from the earth lifting the trees to the heavens. Caroline had become stubborn, arguing with her father that the trees were tall, they were not growing on a mountain! (Henry always became teary at this part of the story). Henry pulled the car over and marched his daughter up a trail, showing her that indeed the mountain was real, the trees were no taller than any average tree. He was right. Caroline, for her part, refused — even in the face of irrefutable fact — to believe the trees were not The Tallest Trees There Ever Were. Henry decided to let the debate go. The pair climbed back into the car and traveled east toward Abe.

Marian never had a part in that story (or in any of Grandpa Henry's stories). She never made a cameo appearance, she never had an opinion or argued with her daughter, or sided with Henry. She never laughed at a funny thing her daughter said or helped Caroline plant a seed, learn to bake, or hunt rabbits. Those were Grandpa Henry's stories. In Henry's den, snuggled in his big chair her grandfather's arms wrapped around her, her small hands holding her mother's photo, Henry had created a nest for Tessa, a safe place where stories of her mother were preserved and protected from Marian's influence. Eventually, the stories stopped. Tessa had never contemplated why, she had assumed as a young girl it was because she had done something wrong. Now as an adult she realized that it was more likely that Marian happened.

Whether she had directly told Henry to stop, or Henry became afraid Tessa was old enough to repeat his stories, either way, Tessa lost the one connection she had to her mother and one of the only pleasures she had growing up. The weight and warmth of Grandpa Henry's arms around her had gotten her through many cold and lonely nights, before and after she left Chapel Corners. She would give anything to feel that weight again now.

It's been a long time since she's seen the sunset from this side of the lake. *I don't even know what I'm doing here*, she thinks. She only knew she could not stand in her office for one more second; the walls that had always brought her comfort closed in on her — Roger Lanford's phone call had stolen her ability to take a deep breath. And Lucy. She stood there looking at her, wondering. It was cliché, she knew. Tess simply couldn't do it any longer.

She had no idea what to do once she got to Chapel Corners. If she was honest, she would admit that she was afraid to set foot in The Corners without a plan. She needed a plan for how to handle Roger Lanford and Marian's death, and a plan to get out. A plan to go back home — to Chicago — and resume her life forgetting this interruption ever happened. Her mind was a cloudy soup of memories, emotions and questions. Did she want to go back to Front Street? Is that why she had run from CH&E and headed straight north? Or did she run because that's what she knows how to do? Run.

There were small turnoffs on the side of the highway all along the coast of the lake; places to picnic, walk your dog, see the dunes or catch a glimpse of the magnificent water. Tess pulled her car into a small cove anchored on the side of the road, pulled a sweatshirt out of her gym bag and kicked off her heels. She walked through the narrow path toward the beach, tiptoeing through the aisle of prickly beach grass twenty yards toward the nippy water. Lake Michigan is the only one of the five Great Lakes that is solely in the United States, which also made it the largest freshwater lake in the country. Tess shook her head as these facts came to her in shards of memory as she sat on the shore of the lake where she had spent so much time growing up. *Maybe if I sit here long enough I will figure out what to do*, she thought.

The sun was sinking under the horizon, spreading colors from peach to pink across the end of the earth. Tess dug her bare feet further into the winter chilled sand; the weight on her toes is grounding (although her hands don't seem to stop shaking). The warm breeze washed over her face and shoulders, taking with it the hard angles of winter that she carried on her shoulders and leaving behind hints of the soft, sloping curves of her agile, summer self. The surf licked the sand gently with lazy, end-of-the-day waves. Despite the shakiness of her hands and the tension across her brow, Tess began to feel still. There is something about the magnitude of the water that centers her, a moment of mindfulness, of the gentle, fading sun, the thick, welcoming sand and the warm breeze carrying a hint of summer's hand allowed her to be quiet for a moment despite where she was and why she was there.

Downtown Chapel Corners was only two miles up

the road. She marveled at the absence of the intrusive sounds of the city she had grown accustomed to in Chicago. There were no sirens, cars, tires, people, or construction here. Tess had left The Corners quickly as a young woman, in a frantic search for a different life. The buzz of the city had thrilled her when she arrived. The sounds of Chicago had symbolized opportunity, change, distance from her past and the pain in it. The energy of the streets and the neighborhoods had helped to create a cocoon for Tess, protecting, nurturing and creating her new life. When you are moving constantly and there are distractions at every turn, it is easier to hide from truths you don't want to acknowledge. The city was her home now, she was comfortable in its chaos and rhythms. Still, as she sat in the sand on the edge of the same water that rolls on the coast in Chicago, she realized she could not appreciate the stillness when she was young.

Looking down the beach, she notices a man throwing a Frisbee out in the water for his golden retriever to fetch. He is wearing a white T-shirt and jeans cuffed at the bottom and his dog is barking loudly, jumping and flailing around – the dog is excited to play. He looks like a normal guy with a normal dog living a normal life. He smiled at Tess as he threw the Frisbee, the dog tearing off into the freezing water with abandon. Envy crept into her thoughts like a spider spinning a web. She fantasized for a moment about joining them, throwing the Frisbee, laughing and playing with the man and his dog. As hard as Tess has worked in her life — and she has worked *tirelessly* — there is a small place in her heart that will never be satisfied. There is an ache that will never be soothed. A deep breath consumed Tess. She looked at the sun setting on the horizon of the lake. Was it so awful to want simple? To want to work hard, have a man to love, have a job that provides? Did everything have to return to the past that she had run from so earnestly? Was it so awful to want to run off into the horizon with normal guy and his normal dog?

Leaving Chapel Corners abruptly and with such conviction has made this sudden change in Tess's daily routine almost commonplace. As bizarre as it was to sit on the beach outside Chapel Corners, as much as she would have laughed if anyone had told her this morning that she would end the day in Michigan, she had always known she would be back. Her return was largely anti-climactic; without expectation there is no anticipation. Without Henry and Marian, there really wasn't much to return to.

Tess wandered through the streets of The Corners in her mind. She had not visited Front Street (where her childhood home stood) in her mind in over a decade. She wondered now, for the first time, how Marian died. Had she been alone? At home? Had she suffered a long illness? Would the home be neglected? Or would the typical order of Marian Wallace have been maintained all these years? Tess contemplated guilt. Marian was her grandmother. She had raised her, clothed her, fed her. Tess was not neglected. Not physically anyway. Rolling Marian's death around in her mind brought her no pain, until she met with Grandpa Henry's memory. Grandpa

Henry.

Tess's hands continued to shake as they had for five hours of her drive north, despite the quiet space she had found on the beach. The underlying anxiety of returning to Chapel Corners was still present. Tessa had become a lawyer because of the rigor of the rules, the predictability of the law and the justice in righting wrongs and creating equality. Not that she did much that impacted society with her work at CH&E. Her pie-in-the-sky idea of what a career in law would be was a far cry from what she did every day. Still, she believed in the foundations of justice, she built a life on them in efforts to insulate herself from the unfairness of the world. Being a lawyer gave Tess a system to believe in, a solid basis for making decisions and guiding hard choices. Had Tess not grown up with Marian Wallace as a grandmother, she may not have been drawn to the justice system as a profession. She was driven toward justice; in a tangible way she could credit her career, or at least the direction of it, to Marian. A familiar pang of fight-or-flight-adrenaline shoot through her. Marian would get no credit from Tess for anything except the stale environment she had grown up in. That and the fact that Marian's last words to her had saddled her with the greatest sadness of her life.

There are a few people walking the beach besides Normal Guy with the dog. Michiganders, much like Chicago natives, crawl out from under rocks and shade their eyes from the long-hidden sun when the warm wind starts to blow. Most of the beachgoers had jackets on and jeans rolled up around their ankles so they could walk in the gently rolling surf. Tonight, the weather holds promise; soon we would rise out of the end of the deep freeze and toward the light of summer. Another deep breath in an attempt to calm her shaking hands, the absence of the smell of gas, the exhaust from passing trucks and the air that blew scents of Indian, Tai and Italian food in your path were noticed. The air here was filled with the smells of the earth: wet rocks and water, dirt, sand and grass. It's been said that the sense of smell is the most powerful of all five senses in recalling memories and evoking emotions. Tess sat with her toes tucked under the sand, the smells of nature, the lake, the sand surrounding her and she held the weight of Grandpa Henry's memory.

When Tess was six years old Grandpa Henry gave her a ring. It was the first grown-up gift she had ever received and she had coveted it. It was simple in design, a small, round turquoise stone embedded in a wreath of sterling silver. Tess wore the ring for years, changing from her ring finger to her pinky as she grew. One hot July day after Henry had passed away Tess was swimming in the lake and it slipped off her finger. Tess didn't notice until she laid down on a large beach blanket with Sarah Beth McGinney, Tess's best friend from kindergarten until she graduated from Chapel Corners High School. The girls searched the sand around the blanket in vain, they borrowed goggles from a pair of middle school aged brothers building sand castles next to them and searched the rolling water. The ring was gone and Tess was heartbroken. Tess smiled now, seeing her ring as a perfectly clear memory in her mind. Her ring had happily bounced along the bottom of the lake, it had rolled and tumbled with the tornadic churning of the waves. Tess imagined by now her ring was lying beneath the layers and layers of sand slowly becoming the permanent bottom of one of the greatest lakes on earth.

Marian and Henry Wallace were married for thirty-three years before he died in an explosion at the shipyard where he worked. Tess had been eleven years old. He had survived the initial explosion with only minor injuries. Henry Wallace then turned around and went back into the flames to save two other co-workers. The three of them were lost. Marian had never cried in Tess's presence. Their marriage was an enigma, Tess could never understand why Henry had married Marian. By the time Tessa entered their lives, Marian was aloof and humorless while Henry was engaging and funny. She was never and he was sometimes. She was peas and dry mashed potatoes, he was ice cream and fried chicken. Cordial and respectful of each other's lives and beings, they were nothing if they were not tepid.

Grandpa Henry loved Lake Michigan. He would take Tess to Castle Pharmacy and Soda Shop for ice cream once a week. The pair would wander down Superior Avenue and walk along the edge of the land, that soggy place where your footprints are erased by a sweep of a wave. Tessa loved those afternoons when she had her grandfather all to herself, where she was free to be a child. To be a little girl. To be silly and funny and spill her ice cream. To Tess, Henry was magic, she believed he could do anything. Tess fantasized their getaway, dreaming of walking straight out into the water. Henry and Tess would hold hands and walk and talk until they were underwater, living like fish. They would be free of Marian, of the shipyard and of Caroline's ghost. Caroline's memory was the only thing that clouded Henry's eyes, and even then her grandfather didn't allow the pain to settle. Tess never knew the story of her mother's death until her final fight with Marian. The truth still hurt Tess.

Tess watched the sun sink toward the horizon and laughed out loud at herself. Tonight the sun looked like a giant glass bead, brilliant in layers of fiery color. Purple, pink and light blue bled out from the center like a Chinese fan. She can't believe she had forgotten about the Sunset Game; quickly she made a guess and counted the time it took from the second the bottom edge touched the water until the crown slipped under. Henry had made the game up as they sat and watched the sunset one evening. He always let her win. It's funny how those little things you do on any given Tuesday don't carry much weight, until you find yourself on any other given Tuesday wishing with all your being to have that boring, basic, typical, normal-every-day-moment back. The Sunset Game. Tessa wished she had remembered it before tonight. She made a quick mental note to play the game in Henry's honor the next time she watched the sunset. Then she remembered she wasn't a person who watched sunsets, and that sadness settled on her shoulders like a wet towel.

Sitting on this slice of beach had started a watershed of memories. Not the large, intrusive, bullying memories she was skilled at suppressing from Chapel Corners, but instead the subtle, gentle pieces of her young life that were hidden in the shadows. These sweet reminders that the pain had forced her away from Chapel Corners did not make up the totality of her past or her memories there. Tess remembered Sarah Beth's mom telling the girls the evening of their high school graduation that life was like a necklace. The big events, the ones we measure ourselves and our success by were the beads: graduations, weddings, births. They made the necklace pretty, when people complimented others on their lives it was the beads they spoke of. What you should compliment someone on was the links that held the beads, the chain on which the beads were strung. The Mondays when you made brownies, or the Wednesday evening where you drank margaritas with your friends, the Saturday night you spent reading every last page of your favorite book or the Sunday morning sermon that made you weep with belief are where the strength of your life resides. The strength is in the chain. Tess sighed and ran her fingers through her hair, tousling her curls. The lavender hour was heavy now, the time after the sun set and before the light of the day has followed her lead. The air around you glows and everything becomes still. In all the stillness, Tess could hear her chain breaking.

Chapter Seven

Tessa stayed on the beach until well after sunset. Damp and cold, she returned to her car to find she had three missed calls and four texts on her cell phone. Three texts from Adrianna, one from Lucy, two calls from Adrianna, and one from Davis. *Davis.* Tess scrambled to see if he had left a message; he hadn't. Adrianna, however, had left two three-minute messages. Tessa deleted both. She answered Lucy quickly: *All good. Be back in office Wednesday.* She powered down her phone after she texted Lucy. It was safer to turn off her life in Chicago for a while.

Tess had three problems to attend to: 1) no place to sleep, 2) no clothes, 3) the shaking in her hands had not calmed but instead spread through her body like a tsunami as the seeds of a migraine sprouted deep in her head. Actually, four problems: she didn't have her migraine medication with her. First things first, a bed for the night.

Main Street in Chapel Corners was dark and quiet. Tess noticed a new Walgreens on the corner of Main and Michigan, her brow furrowed, she hoped that the hometown Castle Pharmacy and Soda Shop wasn't gone. After Henry died, she continued to go to Castle, albeit not as often. In high school she and Sarah Beth would stop in. Sarah Beth always ordered a chocolate malt and

Tessa a strawberry shake. They would sit at the peachy-orange Formica countertop and work on homework. Tess loved the chrome stools with black vinyl fabric seats. The seat all the way to the left had a tear in the middle, they never sat on that one. The walls were covered in old black and white photos of movie stars from the fifties and sixties, and behind the counter was a small television that played those actors' films. The old parlor held an essence of Henry for Tessa, as sweet as the strawberry shakes she loved. She would get a shake there tomorrow before she went home, she decided.

The streetlights were new. Stately, with three lantern-style arms, they added charm to the small downtown. An independent coffee shop was now on the main drag, Cup of Joe looked interesting. As she drove down the darkened street, there were a few novelty shops that Tess didn't remember, one with a nautical theme, another a baby boutique and the last a small bookstore. The old Sun Theatre had been renovated (when she lived here you were stuck with the choice of one-season-old movie and now there were four new releases!). Where once a small sign had hung in the front, now a large white marquee lit up the night. Tess looked ahead, spying the familiar golden arches — McDonald's had finally found Chapel Corners.

Tess came to the four corners in the center of town. In the middle of the charming downtown there were four churches, one on each corner. The Catholics were on the southeast with a big, beautiful stone building, and the Baptists on the southwest with a smaller, white building with a red door and red shutters on the windows. The Methodist church had been remodeled in the 1970s and was on the northeast corner. The northwest corner was a non-denominational church that was a small brick chapel. It was simple and elegant, it had always been Tessa's favorite. There was no denying it, she was back in Chapel Corners.

She turned north and drove between the Methodist and non-denominational church toward the only motel she could remember in town, The Waterside Inn. Although technically not waterside, you could see a view of the lake if you stood just right in the parking lot, and there was a path off the main sidewalk out front that lead you down to the beach. There were likely new hotels on the highway running out of town, but the sight of the Waterside comforted Tess. If not a friendly memory, it was at least familiar on a day that was full of the unfamiliar.

Vacancy. *Thank God.*

Tess shifted her car into park and settled back into her seat. An afternoon of driving had landed her a decade into the past and her body ached with fatigue. The last fifteen minutes in the car, Tess hatched a plan. At eight a.m. she would visit Robert Lanford, ask him to prepare a renunciation relieving her of the duty as executor of Marian's estate. She would make a quick visit to the house where she grew up, where Marian died, to take with her any and all of Grandpa Henry's things that may still be there. Then, she'll head back to Chicago to deal with CH&E, Davis, and Adrianna. She hadn't decided what she would say about her disappearing act yet. There was a reason she had not shared her past with those in her life now, and that reason had not changed. Adrianna would be more concerned with how Tess's disappearance affected her, so she wouldn't be a problem. She may not even ask where Tessa had been. Tess's work record was exemplary, enough to warrant the benefit of the doubt from Holmes. She doubted he would question her about a private family issue. Davis had accepted vague answers in the past, perhaps he would again. Tess gave herself a gut check. She left Davis's bed two days before she learned about Marian's passing. She hadn't answered Davis's call earlier today, which was their only communication since Saturday. Davis would not be satisfied with ill-defined details of her last forty-eight hours, and he would not be satisfied with no explanation for her leaving Saturday night. Tess's stomach rolled with anxiety, a recognizable gnawing at her conscience. *Davis.*

Tess slung her gym bag out from the back seat and threw it over her shoulder. At least she had a pair of shorts and a T-shirt to sleep in, as well as a much-needed toothbrush. The hotel was a single floor, all the rooms had their own door that opened to the outside. Where it should have been creepy and perhaps suspect, it was quaint, almost artistic. In the summertime there was rarely vacancy. It had become a legacy hotel to many families, having opened in 1947. Families from around the Midwest visited for generations, enjoying Chapel Corners and the Waterside Inn, an idyllic destination that time had forgotten. Tess collected her purse from the front seat and gathered it with her gym bag. She headed into the front lobby, the door jingled with the sound of bells alerting the clerk to a customer. Tess's head squeezed at the jarring noise as she looked around the small but charming room.

A blue couch circa late 1970s and two armchairs that weren't much younger stood in the corner. Tess's overwhelming fatigue begged her to sit and wait for the help. Sepia toned and black and white pictures of Chapel Corners as it once was lined the back wall. Underneath each photograph was a small brass plaque both dating and locating the shot; the earliest Tess saw dated back to 1846.

Her gaze scanned each picture on the wall, taking in the scene as if it were a place she had never been. Folks around here were proud of The Corners and the town's commitment to keeping to its roots, not conforming to change. Tessa stopped at a picture of the McGinney Orchard, 1967. The familiar farmhouse was set deep on the hill overseeing her groves of trees. Tears came to Tess's eyes, gently, without fanfare. If there was happiness to be found in this small town, one would find it in the beautiful trees that lined the McGinney Orchard.

Sarah Beth and her family owned McGinney Orchard. Tess spent hours with her best friend under the gnarled, twisting trunks of those old apple trees. Springtime was her favorite at the orchard, the smell of apple was heavy in the air, along with the promise of long summer days as a reward in the months to come. Sara Beth and Tessa would lie on their backs underneath the spider's web of branches looking up at the pink and white blossoms.

"I don't want to go home," Tessa would say.

"I know," Sarah Beth would answer.

Tessa hadn't thought about Sarah Beth in years. They had been so close, more like sisters than best friends. Tessa shook her head at the loss, their friendship another casualty of Tessa cutting all ties to Chapel Corners. Guilt accompanied Tess's tears. She rarely had physical reactions to feelings, her body long ago learning to separate and protect. She had learned from Marian, if emotions stayed academic they were manageable. It's when they became visceral, when you felt them in your gut and in your heart and in your bones that they became too strong to control. Tess had become skilled at stalling her emotions where they could be handled.

"Hello there, can I help you?" An older woman, short and round in a Mrs. Claus kind of way, wearing a gauzy purple scarf tied around her neck with pleasant blue-gray hair in ringlets close to her head greeted Tessa at the counter. "Reenie" was printed on the faded gold background of the rectangle name tag that hung from her shirt.

Tess turned away from the hall of history, a thin smile stretched across her face. "Hi there. I need a room, please." Weariness dripped from every word.

"Of course, dear. You look like you need a room." Reenie's eyes blessed Tessa with warmth and kindness.

Reenie worked quickly to input Tess's name and address into the computer as Tessa rifled through her purse for her credit card. Tess squinted and shielded her eyes with her hand, saluting toward Reenie and the fluorescent bulbs hanging above the counter. Tessa placed her credit card on the counter. "How many nights do you need the room?" Reenie asked.

"Just one, please."

"Where are you coming from?"

"Chicago." *Didn't I just give her my address?* Tess thought.

"What brought you to our neck of the woods?" Reenie asked. Tessa grabbed her head with her free hand, squeezing her temples, trying in vain to release the pressure that was building already.

"Business," Tess answered quickly.

Reenie nodded her head "Ahh..." she answered. It occurred to Tessa that Reenie may have recognized her name, but the thought flew out as quickly as it landed. Tess was too tired to worry about that now.

"Okay, if you could just initial here next to your rate and sign over here for your card." The pleasant woman looked at Tess's credit card and signature. "Tessa Wallace. Are you Marian Wallace's granddaughter?"

The mere mention of Marian's name sent spikes flying around Tess's already swollen and irritated brain. "Yes, I am Henry and Marian Wallace's granddaughter."

"Oh my, dear. I am so sorry about your grandmother. Marian and I were in the woman's church group together for years, we also bowled together up at Paradise Lanes in the Wednesday afternoon Lunch Ladies' League."

"Thank you for your sympathies."

"Your grandfather Henry was a good man."

Lightening her grip on the pen still in her hand, Tess let it fall to the counter. "Yes he was, thank you." Tess's voice was quiet.

"Okay, dear. Here you go. Room 111. Right down the end here, in the morning you can see the lake from the corner of the window in that room."

"Thank you."

"Do you need help with your bags?"

"No, thank you, I can carry what I need." Tess turned and walked in the direction Reenie pointed, desperate for quiet darkness.

The room was small and clean, sparsely furnished but decorated tastefully, if not up to date. The old-fashioned furnishings didn't offend or turn Tessa off. Instead Tess was comforted. There were two double beds, a nightstand between the two, bolted to the wall, and a television stand across the room with a small TV placed in the larger opening. A desk lined the wall near a window that was treated in simple purple drapes. The carpet was a soft green and relatively new, with a shallow pile. There were only two lights in the room, one being overhead. Tessa tossed her gym bag on one bed and crawled slowly under the covers of the opposite bed. Purple gladiolas and green leaves covered the blanket.

Lying there it occurred to Tess that Reenie offered condolences upon Marian's death, but offered thoughts of affection for her Grandpa Henry, a man dead for nearly twenty years. Marian had been skillful in her general disregard for Tessa, showing her just enough attention in public to push aside any fears that a young

Tessa was unhappy, as well as send highly mixed messages to her granddaughter as to what would make Marian happy. It comforted Tessa to think maybe some people in this town saw through the façade that Marian Wallace carefully constructed.

Tess sifted through a pile of take-out menus: pizza, Mexican, Chinese. She called the Mexican restaurant first, a big, sloppy wet burrito sounded perfect, but they were closed early. Garden Lee Chinese's menu said it was open until ten. She called, placed her order and headed out to get her food. Davis loved Tess's appetite, he laughed that she out-ate him pound for pound. He said it was refreshing to take a woman out and have her not only order up what she wanted, but enjoy eating it. Tess picked up her sweet and sour chicken, two egg rolls and sticky rice and stopped by the Walgreens to grab a cheap bottle of wine, Excedrin Migraine, a Clif bar and orange juice for the morning. She threw face wash and lotion in as well.

Tess flipped through channels while eating dinner, tucked under the homespun comforter. She drank the mediocre Merlot from a plastic cup, the wine warming her belly as quickly as the food filled it. Nothing held her attention for long. She watched fifteen minutes of the cult classic *Can't Buy Me Love* with Patrick Dempsey, another ten minutes watching Andrew Zimmern on *Bizarre Foods* (she turned that channel when Andrew ate grilled intestines in Mexico). She tried *Beachfront Bargain Hunt* on HGTV, where two college sweethearts were looking for a beachfront surf shack in Costa Rica had just started. Tess stalled her channel surfing again.

Of all the adventures Tess and Davis had been on, Jaco Beach in Costa Rica was hands down her favorite. They rode horses in the jungle, fed toucans and monkeys from their hands, saw parakeets on long walks in the rain forests and crossed over a bridge where hundreds of crocodiles lay resting beneath them in the Tarcoles River. They rode four-wheelers in the mountains and spent a day (one of her all-time best days) surfing on Jaco Beach.

Clouds covered the sky in putty-colored puffs, rain came and went like a gentle baptism, the sun peeking out to warm your shoulders just as your skin bloomed in goosebumps. The sea stretched out in a wide expanse, like the Montana sky. Davis and Ryan had spent every break during college finding new waves to surf, they ventured to Australia, New Zealand and Hawaii and considered briefly opening a surfing school in Honduras before coming home to Chicago. Davis was excited for Tess to experience the sea this way. He scheduled a private lesson for Tessa with a young man named, predictably, Jose. She practiced on dry land, striking surfing poses on her board while it sat cradled in the sand like a boat on a lift. When she and Jose swam out into the water for her first waves, the rain started again. The mixture of salty sea and fresh rain dripping down her cheeks and wetting her mouth was sweet. She remembered the gritty sand scrapping her hips when she fell off the board and tumbled underwater, bouncing off the bottom, the pure joy of commanding a wave and riding for a few seconds. The anticipation, poised and ready watching her wave come closer, listening to Jose's commands, was thrilling. It was, by far, the most physically challenging thing she ever tried. Tess was never much of an athlete. She swam on the swim team in high school like her mother had done, though she never found the success Caroline had in the pool. Now, she exercised because she was supposed to. She went to spin class, did yoga when she could fit it in, ran on occasion with Davis when he asked. But this… Surfing was the perfect marriage of challenge: physical and mental. When she surfed her legs were strong, her core was tough and she was brave. It was her against the sea, her against the waves, amongst the hovering mountains and never-ending water. It was beautiful, spiritual, and she loved it.

When she was done, bone-tired, chilled despite the warm air, and full of salt water in her belly, she dragged herself from the water. The weight of her body pressed her back down to earth. She and Davis rinsed off quickly under makeshift showers and harder rains. They found the first beach bar on the right and tucked themselves into a booth for the night. They drank margaritas and ate what they both agreed were the best fish tacos they ever had. The day melted into a perfect evening, Tess was grateful for the rain, the rain that blessed them. More than the euphoria that comes with a perfect vacation day, Tess felt free. Free to be herself. Free to be the person she had worked so hard to become, despite her hidden past. She was content, settled and happy. Marian and Chapel Corners felt a lifetime away. In Jaco Beach she had been protected from her past by her future.

Her thumb clicked, quickly changing the channel. As wonderful as the memories were, they were an illusion. Jaco Beach had been at the beginning of her relationship with Davis, the freedom was make-believe. They were just starting to learn about each other and what Tess saw as a safe space, Davis saw as the beginning of a longer road to sharing confidences, stories, histories. He was never interested in staying on Jaco Beach, he wanted to move forward.

Tess pulled herself from under her covers, gathered her trash from takeout and shoved it into the plastic delivery bag. Two fortune cookies settled in the bottom of the bag caught her eye. She cracked open the first one, stripping the paper from between the wafers. "Be on the lookout for coming events; they cast their shadows beforehand." Goosebumps spread down Tess's arms, just like they had on Jaco Beach. The shadows were what she was afraid of.

Chapter Eight

The orange light read 5:57 and broadcast near morning across the hotel room. Tess had fallen asleep quickly, thanks to the long drive and cheap Walgreens merlot. Around one a.m. the effects of the wine had worn off and Tess had seen every hour turn since. Six o'clock was reasonable enough to climb out of bed, she decided. She searched through her gym bag, pulled out a pair of yoga pants, sports bra and shirt, got dressed and slipped outside to get her mat from the Volvo.

The path down to the lake was sand, scattered with small stones, sticks, pinecones and prickly beach grass. One of the things Tess had loved best about Michigan beaches was the pine trees that grew in the dunes and the edges of the sand. Not at all what one expected when they thought of a beach getaway, Michigan beaches were unique. "Ouch!" Tess whispered as a small stick landed in the soft flesh of her right arch. She hadn't bothered with putting on her tennis shoes, choosing instead to walk barefoot down to the water. She held her mat close to her chest. The darkness and unfamiliar terrain made her breath come quicker and her palms slipped against the rubber of the mat. Cold sand softened against the strike of her steps, waves crashed up ahead. She was nearly there.

The trees, mostly pine, had made a tunnel over the trail that opened up at the beach. Tess looked left and right, deciding to walk north, away from the public beach that was accessible from downtown and not far from where she stood. No one was likely to be out this early, the sun wouldn't be up for another hour, although the sky was waking with dusty light. The purple mat clung to itself as she tried to roll it out. She tamped the corners down in the sand. Rolling her body from bottom to head one vertebra at a time as she had been taught, her back settled into the mat. She used her shoulder blades to form a cove to make herself comfortable. Arms stretched over her head she took a deep breath, in and out, and repeated it.

Years ago when she began her yoga practice she had been afraid that it would be boring, that her brain would wander and she would spend the entire class creating a To-Do list in her mind. What she found was that her time on the mat was the only time her brain wasn't churning. The movements looked simple, but their execution was not. Tess preferred to practice in a class, allowing her body and brain to routinely follow the instructor's gentle commands, "Shoulders down, Tessa… Tuck your bottom under your hips, Tessa… Knee over the heel, there you go." It was a pleasure to follow directions, to be in charge of nothing except compliance, to make no decisions.

She began with sun salutations, standing in mountain pose and drawing in several breaths. Her body took over as her mind turned inward and focused on her breath, in and out, in and out. Warmth built in her belly, four sun salutations were complete. The pace was slow and deliberate, waves crept toward her mat in sync with her movements. She continued with the same poses, choosing to keep things simple. Tess sped up her pace and she worked through Surya Namaskar numbers seven and eight. Her shirt clung to her skin and draped crooked across her shoulders. Having lost count of how many salutations she had completed, she finally lay in Savasana, corpse pose. Her measured breath fell away, waves lapped in a distant consciousness and Tess wept. The sunlight met her tears as it rose through the pines and peeked out between their needled branches.

Déjà vu descended on Tessa, a heady feeling of nostalgia mixed with surrender. Tessa spent the first part of her life under Marian's rule and her entire adult life running from her, yet here she was in Chapel Corners and Marian was gone. Marian may have been her grandmother, but she raised her as a mother would. Marian had fed her, clothed her, demanded good grades. Her physical needs were met. It was the intangibles a mother gave that had been neglected. Marian was utilitarian, disciplined. She never tucked Tessa in or braided her hair, she didn't teach her to bake or ask her to help with dinner. They didn't hold hands and walk down the street or sit and watch television together. She was not a confidant nor a safe place to fall. Marian gave orders, kept things organized and was militant about rules. There were the comments, the "Marianisms" as she and Sarah called them. "Tessa, you don't need another helping." "Tessa, you can't take Advanced Algebra, you won't pass it." "Tessa, children are to be seen and not heard." It wasn't until their final argument that Marian had become outright cruel. Before that, Marian's barbs were disguised as parenting.

As a young girl, Tessa was fascinated with mother-daughter relationships. She followed moms hauling kids in their carts and ones who held their children's hands through the grocery store. She eavesdropped on their conversations and watched how mothers touched their daughters' arms, held their hands and kissed their heads. She read books about mothers and daughters and took quizzes in *Seventeen* magazine, "How Close to Your Mom are You?" and "Find Out if You Will Turn Out Just Like Your Mom!" Her answers were make-believe, and she was wistful when the results were "Your mom is your BFF!" and "You and your mom are twins." How she wished for that to be true.

Tessa and Sarah Beth had spent hours crying over the movie *Steel Magnolias*. Sarah Beth loved Julia Roberts, Tess loved how much M'Lynn loved Shelby. She studied M'Lynn as she would have prepared for an English paper. M'Lynn gazed at her daughter in a way that made Tessa's heart ache. In the end, Shelby died, and Tessa was jealous. Shelby had the one thing that Tessa never did. The love and care of a mother. Henry tried to fill the gap, to warm the spot in her soul that was empty. The place where the love from Tess's mother should have lived.

Tessa dreaded Mother's Day. Marian, by default, received a Mother's Day card that Henry took Tessa to Castle Pharmacy to buy. They coupled it with a package of Russell Stover Mint Dream candy and a rose from the bucket at the counter. Henry and Tess took Marian to brunch at the Family Tree Cafe. Tess would order their homemade cinnamon roll and Marian would scoff, "Are you sure that's what you should eat?" Henry would smile at Tess and share the cinnamon role with her.

After Tess was tucked into bed, Henry and Marian safely downstairs, Tess wrote a note every year to her mother, her *real* mother, on Mother's Day. Tess knew so little about Caroline, these letters gave her the freedom to fantasize about who she would have been. She would have always been kind, and fun! She would have been so much fun! They would have baked apple pies together like Sarah Beth did with Mrs. McGinney, they would have hiked to the top of the Sleeping Bear Dunes — just the two of them — and run down arms and legs akimbo as they screamed and laughed, barreling toward the water. They would have ridden bikes on Mackinac Island and taken the ferry from Covington across the big lake to Milwaukee with Uncle Henry to see the Tigers play the Brewers. Tess dreamed about planting daffodils and growing tomatoes. She would have confided in her mother about boys and told her all about Dana Seltzer who was the designated Mean Girl in middle school. Caroline would have had the best advice. Tess would have never gone to bed without hearing her momma say she was smart and beautiful and strong.

When Tess had arrived at Northwestern just after her eighteenth birthday, she had been elated. Eighteen was magical, the age when she would be in charge and Marian could no longer hold her thumb over Tess's neck. However, a mother-daughter relationship was created in many ways. Tess spent her life mourning the mother she never knew and resenting the one she was given. Now, she realized, that regardless how she willed her mother to be Caroline, her mother in this life was Marian. No matter the distance in miles or years, Marian would always have her thumb over Tess's neck because she allowed it.

Although it was a warmer May than most, Tess's sweaty skin chilled by the big lake breeze signaled it was time to go. Gauging the time by the rise of the sun, she pulled herself upright, sitting cross-legged on her mat, hands rested on top of her lap. The murky light had given way to a brighter morning in the past hour. Tess saw a man running down the beach, moving quickly toward her. The man, in his mid-forties, wore shorts and a Ferris State University T-shirt. His eye caught Tess's as he continued his pace, his smile was kind. "Good morning," he said.

"Good morning…" Tess quipped in return. The man continued to run, his footfalls landed in time with the waves. *So strange,* Tess thought. Eleven years was a long time in some ways, and a heartbeat in others. The beach, the lake, even the runner, were all familiar. Smoothing out a canvas in the sand she traced the letters spelling Henry's name with tip of her index finger, then wrote hers underneath. *So strange,* she repeated in her mind. She stood up, rolled her purple mat, leaving the sand that clung to the bottom for another time.

Tess slugged down the orange juice and Clif bar and

chased it with two Excedrin Migraine tablets. Her skirt and blouse had hung in the bathroom while she showered in hopes of hanging out the creases from half a day's work and the long drive. Finger combing her hair (she should have grabbed a brush at Walgreens!) she pulled it up into a make-shift ponytail and brushed her teeth. First she would run to the coffee shop she saw up the road to gather her thoughts before she headed to Roger Lanford's office.

Inside Joe to Go was dark in contrast to the hazy sunlight of the late May morning. The unseasonably warm weather they had been having in Chicago the past few days had followed Tess across the lake. Tess smiled as she imagined the warm weather sweeping behind her from her new life in Chicago in the colors of a rainbow. The vision strengthened her resolve that she could complete her task and make it home with her life intact. She deserved that. Grandpa Henry always said if you didn't like the weather, stick around for ten minutes it will change. Michigan is like that, especially here by the lake; she remembered that now. The confidence conjured by the warm weather and imaginary rainbow teetered.

There were two large leather chairs the color of caramel, with cushions that billowed like marshmallows sitting on either side of a gas fireplace. Five tables were sprinkled through the room, with seating and a bar that lined the area where the baristas worked. Brick red paint covered the walls, and the ceiling was lined in gold tin. The building was long and narrow, reminding her of the General Store at Greenfield Village. Tessa had visited the

Henry Ford Museum and Greenfield Village in Dearborn in fifth grade. She had loved the General Store, a long, narrow building filled with goods that had been sold during the turn of the century. She coveted the delicate and detailed hair clips, the combs and the ladies' shoes. Sarah Beth was fascinated with the women's hats and small packages of soap.

Tessa and Sarah Beth had been the only girls in their class that stayed for the entire glass blowing demonstration. The workers repeated a cycle of heating and blowing and heating and blowing until a Christmas ornament emerged. The end product was a ruby red teardrop swirled with purple, green, gold and white. Tessa thought it was beautiful. Grandpa Henry had secretly tucked money into her coat pocket before she left that morning to buy a souvenir. Tessa bought her treasure. Eight months later she covered the ornament in wrapping paper she had made in Mrs. Mattson's art class and gave it to Marian for Christmas. It was the winter before Henry died. Marian unwrapped it and smiled. Tessa felt a sliver of warm sunshine on her shoulders that morning. Marian liked the gift. *Where did that memory come from?* she thought now.

Tessa ordered her standard, tall chai tea skinny and a cinnamon roll, and picked up a copy of *The Chapel Corners Gazette* from a pile at the cash register. Her high school journalism class was given a weekly column that rotated between the students. Each student submitted an article on Monday for the following Friday's paper. Mr. Banks, the journalism teacher and advisor for the school newspaper and yearbook, was careful to highlight each student at least once. Tess had been chosen three times her senior year. Her submissions had been chosen more often than anyone in class. Tess had never wanted to be a lawyer, she had wanted to be a writer.

It had been Mr. Banks who had helped her apply to Northwestern her senior year. Marian knew nothing about it, and Tess had not asked for her advice or help with any of the details. She had been determined to do it on her own.

Tess burned her tongue taking an early sip from her tea. "Dammit!" she cursed quietly. She was waiting for her toasted cinnamon roll to be delivered to her cozy seat. Her phone was still off this morning, although it was settled at the bottom of her purse. With no Facebook or Twitter or Instagram to distract her, she surveyed her surroundings, surprised to be enjoying being untethered from her phone. There was a couple sitting in the corner, sharing a piece of what looked like the blueberry crumble muffin she almost ordered. They were holding hands and whispering. Tessa noticed the sign hanging on the wall above the corner table, "Nobody puts baby in a corner" and smiled. She missed Davis. A young man in the opposite corner scribbled furiously inside a black and white marbled notebook. He does not stop to think or ponder. His pen has not stopped carving words on paper since Tess sat down. Tess envies the young man, the freedom to uncensor his thoughts and just write.

Tess pulled out a notebook from her purse then scrounged for a pen at the bottom, skimming her phone with her fingers. Tess loved lists. She had lists of To-Dos at work, To-Dos at her apartment, she had Five-Year To-Dos and Lifetime To-Dos. She supposed the five year and lifetime lists were more accurately termed "goals," but Tess preferred to write them as action items, not dreams or far-off goals. She was far more likely to complete a To-Do list, she reasoned. Tessa was known to write an item down on a To-Do list even after she completed the task, just so she could take a Sharpie pen and cross it off. When she was eighteen and left Chapel Corners for good she had constructed a Five-Year To-Do list and one Lifetime To-Do list. The Five-Year list had been completed: 1) graduate college, 2) apply and get admitted to law school, 3) never go back to Chapel Corners. She had constructed subsequent Five-Year To-Do lists: 1) finish law school, 2) make partner in ten years, 3) practice yoga, 4) travel to Italy. Her Lifetime To-Do List had two items: marry the love of my life and live happily ever after.

A tall, older gentleman stood in line to order behind two teenage girls. The tilt of his nose in profile seemed familiar. Tess smiled in response to his gaze in her direction. Was he the father of an old classmate? No, he didn't look to be quite that old. Oddly, it hadn't occurred to Tess until now that there would still be people in Chapel Corners that she may know. She had successfully disconnected herself from life here when she left a decade ago. Leaving Marian and their awful fight meant leaving the good things and people in Chapel Corners, like Sarah Beth behind. Tessa was ashamed she had not given much thought to the girl she had always believed would be her lifelong best friend. The bells above the door rang as a young mom came in with her baby in a stroller. Tessa found herself looking to the door, wishing Sarah Beth would walk in. They weren't even Facebook friends, Tessa had no idea if she was still in town or not. She felt a pang of loneliness for Sarah Beth last night when she saw the photos of McGinney's Orchard at the Waterside. Now, that pang has become a dull ache. She missed Sarah Beth. The gentleman in line took another glance in her direction. *He's the runner from the beach!* she realized. No wonder he was glancing at her, they had been in the same place twice already this morning and it was not eight a.m. yet!

To Do List for today:

    1) speak with Lanford

    2) complete renunciation

    3) go to Front Street and get Henry's things

    4) call Sarah Beth?

    5) call Davis?

Tessa wavered at numbers four and five. She was not a fan of placing items on a list that she didn't intend to complete, yet she was not confident that she would complete these two. With her To-Do list finished, Tessa smiled again at the runner and turned her attention to the newspaper, tucking her list back into her purse beside her phone.

Peter Restin had a byline on the front page with a thumbnail picture underneath, "New Safety Regulations in Effect at Covington Shipyard." She was fairly sure he was the boy who sat behind Tess in geography in the tenth grade and perpetually twisted his pencil in her hair. She passed the Soviet Union geography unit because Peter had come up with a song to remember the tongue-twister names of every Soviet state in counter-clockwise order. "Estonia and Latvia got married in Lithuania..." Tess couldn't remember the rest, she only remembered the tune. Tessa had written in his yearbook at the senior yearbook dance, "Thanks for all the laughs and the help passing Geo Soph year! Good luck next year!" She scanned the sports section, recognizing last names on a few of the pee-wee baseball players listed. Tess wondered if those athletes were the children of past classmates. An advertisement for Castle Pharmacy was in the bottom right hand corner of the Community page next to an op-ed piece regarding the use of the town hall. She saw a coupon for Garden Lee, the Chinese joint she got takeout from last night, and laughed out loud. Gone for a decade, and not a whole lot has changed in this little town.

The face surprised her. The long, straight nose with a slight bump mid-crest was unmistakable.

Marian's obituary.

The picture the *Gazette* had printed was one that Tessa had not seen before. Marian was older, of course, her eyes turned down just a bit in the corners and her lids drooped. She was angular, as always, a strong jaw jutted forward and a small cleft pierced her chin. Tess searched her eyes. She was not an unattractive woman. Tess had never given thought one way or another to her grandmother's looks. Her beauty had been dampened by her spirit. However, in still life, Marian was almost pretty. She had aged over the past ten years, although not as much as Tess would have thought.

MARIAN WALLACE, age 73, died at home on Tuesday, May 17, 2017. She was preceded in death by her husband Henry Wallace, daughter Caroline Wallace, brother James (Fiona) Sattler, and parents Grace and Terrence Sattler. She is survived by her granddaughter, Tessa Wallace of Chicago, Illinois and several siblings. Mrs. Wallace was a member of the Home Gardening Club, the Ladies Lunch Bowling League as well as the Baptist Church Women's Group. All donations can be made to the Children's Action Organization through The Gardens Funeral Home. At the request of Mrs. Wallace, cremation services were performed and no public service will be held.

Tessa's heart raced. She held onto the bulky ceramic cup with both hands, re-reading the obituary twice more. How does a life become reduced to a paragraph? Outside of being Tess's grandmother, Marian had been a mother and a wife, she had kept a home and gone to church. She had been a sister and a daughter. The bones of her life would have been enough to create a legacy, she could have had the end of her life celebrated by those who loved her, who respected and admired her. Instead, her granddaughter was informed of her death by her lawyer.

Her husband was dead. Her daughter was dead. She had no one. She kept herself from everyone

Tess's future flickered before her eyes. What kind of life was she creating? How would her obituary read? Who would grieve for her life? Who would she be survived by? Tessa knew the answer. Tess had always believed that leaving Chapel Corners had been the right thing to do. Was it? Was cutting out Sarah Beth and her family worth it? Was lying to Davis worth it? Was keeping a circle of friends so small it wasn't even a circle worth it? Was keeping Grandpa Henry and her memories hidden in a place so deep in her soul, she only allowed herself to shine a light on them when no one else could see them worth it? Tess had always believed it was. The end would always justify the means. Doubt crept in like the January wind through a drafty door.

> TESSA WALLACE, age 73, died at home on Tuesday, May 17, 2045. She was preceded in death by her mother, Caroline Wallace, her grandparents, Henry & Marian Wallace. Tessa was a senior partner at Chadwick, Holmes & Epstein, was a member in good standing with the Illinois Real Estate Lawyers Association and the American Bar Association. She contributed yearly to the Children's Action Organization and to the Northwestern School of Law.

Tess folded the paper and tucked it under her arm, left her unfinished tea and half-eaten cinnamon roll on the table next to the marshmallow chair, and left Joe to Go. *Chicago? How did she know I was in Chicago? Why did she know I was in Chicago?* Marian's wish to have donations made to the Children's Action Organization was also perplexing. Did she know Tessa went to college on a scholarship she received from the CAO? Did she know that Tessa was dating Davis and that together they were involved in CAO? She must have. CAO was a large charity organization in the Midwest, but Tess couldn't conceive of a way that Marian would have known about it other than through Tess.

Tess walked quickly, counting her steps in the background of her mind. *One, two, three, four…*

As she walked, she mulled around the knowledge that Marian had been familiar with her life. The better part of her adult life had been spent burying the family she had in Chapel Corners and the legacy they left her with beneath a new facade and new memories and a new life. She had assumed Marian had done the same. It never occurred to Tess that Marian may have wished Tessa hadn't left. It never occurred to her that Marian may have been hurt by her granddaughter's disappearance, or wanted things to be different. It never occurred to her that the remainder of Marian's days had been spent alone. Tess's dull headache roared back again as she walked back to the Waterside to dress and meet with Lanford.

Chapter Nine

Luke Castle sat in his chair, holding on to his cup of coffee from Joe to Go with both hands, anchoring himself to the desk. For years Caroline had come to him in his dreams, always a vision of the girl she was the last time he saw her. Having lost her so young had shaped him. He believed he was less of a man than he would have been had she lived, had they been allowed to grow the family they had created. In his dreams Caroline was happy, she was whole and safe. She came to him when he needed her, she comforted him and brought him peace.

There had been times since her death that Luke thought he saw her in the grocery store, or at the lake. Once he saw her likeness in the Detroit airport when he and his wife Cynthia were flying to Tampa, Florida for vacation. On every occasion he knew his mind was seeking similarities in a stranger with the first woman he had ever loved. Today, first on the beach and then in the coffee shop was something different. He hoped the young woman was not afraid of him, he could hardly keep himself from glancing in her direction. He had been helpless in his desire to see her. He tried to be subtle, although he didn't think he had been successful. Could she be back? Could that have been her today doing yoga on the beach? Drinking coffee at Cup of Joe?

Reaching into the bottom drawer of his desk, Luke pulled out a framed photograph, nearly twenty years old. The little girl in the snapshot was perched on the counter in the ice cream parlor in the back of the pharmacy. She wore a red, plaid gingham dress with a Peter Pan collar and white Mary Janes. A curl had slipped from her braided hair and hung loosely, framing the side of her face. It had been against their agreement to take the photo; his then-girlfriend, now-wife, Cynthia had snapped it quickly while Henry had gone to the bathroom during their weekly visit. For all these years it has been all he had to remember her — and her mother.

Luke had always been grateful to Cynthia for understanding, for being gracious enough to offer no judgment, only kindness and support. This support was one of the reasons he had fallen in love with her, and certainly a cornerstone of why they had been married for two decades. She had been patient with his wounded heart, and allowed Caroline and his daughter to reside there without jealousy. She allowed him the space to continue to remember and honor them, and she loved him as much for his loyalty and commitment to them as his commitment to her. He was lucky, he knew, that she was willing to accept most of him. He was unable to give her all of him. He reached for his phone to call his wife, but stopped short. He was afraid to say the words aloud. He was afraid to hope. After all this time, had his daughter come home?

Chapter Ten

Roger Lanford's office was an old, blue house on Main Street that he converted into an office. A soldier's row of bright yellow daffodils lined the front walk leading to a front porch that sagged in the middle. The Christmas lights hung dormant, draped along the edges of the old house, stapled to the outside just beneath the gutters that needed cleaning. One of Tess's pet peeves: when Christmas is over, it's over. CH&E had elaborate landscaping, window boxes full of beautifully textured greens with pops of color from ever blooming flowers. At Christmas time, the firm was professionally decorated with large white bulbs that hung from level straight wires that were seamlessly tucked out of view. There were huge poinsettias, a magazine worthy Christmas tree stood sentry on every floor and the main fountain in the center of the building was lit with red lights from within. The contrast between CH&E and Lanford and Associates (did he even *have* any associates?) was stark. One deep breath and four stairs were all that stood between Tessa and her past.

"Good morning, I'm here to see Mr. Lanford. Tessa Wallace from Chadwick, Holmes and Epstein." Tessa stated her purpose with authority, adding her own position in hopes that the fact she did not have an appointment would not be an issue. It hadn't occurred to her until now that Roger Lanford could have a full schedule of meetings and court appearances, or maybe had been unable to come to work.

"Good morning, Tessa. It's a beautiful day, isn't it? Do you have an appointment?" answered the soft, round woman sitting at the front desk.

"I don't, Barb," Tessa said beaming her lawyer smile, reading the woman's name off her nameplate on her desk. "My trip to Chapel Corners was unplanned. However, it's imperative that I speak with him today. Is he in?"

"He will be. 9:15. And you are in luck, his first appointment just canceled." Barb smiled a maple-syrup smile backed by more authority than the Chapel Corners Police Department. "You can have a seat, I'll let you know when he's ready for you."

"Thank you so much, I appreciate it." Lucy might be a guard dog at the door, but Barb could hold her own.

Tessa waited in what appeared to be the former living room of the old home, sitting on a hard-backed wooden chair with enough age to call it "antiquated." The office was benign and unimpressive; the walls were dingy yellow and likely hadn't seen a fresh coat of paint since Tessa left town. It smelled of mothballs and stale paper and Tess had an urge to shove open a window. Instead she drummed her fingers on her tapping leg as she waited.

Mr. Lanford arrived to his office at exactly 9:15. He smiled at Tessa, checked in with Barb, and headed toward the back of the building. Ten minutes later Roger emerged once more, this time he said, "Tessa. Roger

Lanford." He offered Tessa his right hand in greeting. "I'm so pleased to see you. Come on back, let's talk in my office." He led Tessa through a conference room (dining room), kitchenette (kitchen), and past a bathroom into his office, tucked away in the far corner.

"Thank you for seeing me on such short notice, Mr. Lanford. I hope I haven't upset your schedule today." As they rounded the corner into Roger's office Tessa took a deep breath and her eyes gaped open. Roger Lanford's office was in squalor. Cobwebs in every corner of the room danced in a gentle draft from the ceiling fan and the age-dulled white walls desperately needed a coat of paint.

And there were piles. They jutted up creating a skyline against the dull white walls that would rival Manhattan. There was a small footpath from the door leading to a guest chair immediately across from his desk, which Tess followed, teetering one towering stack of papers dangerously. The carpet was the color of walnuts and hadn't been vacuumed in months, if ever. Tessa could hear Barb's melodic tapping of the computer keys and briefly wondered not only about the organization of Lanford and Associates but also the confidentiality. Sweet Barb probably had Reenie down at the Waterside on speed dial. Tessa absentmindedly wondered out loud how her grandmother, who was militant about order and cleanliness had ever chosen Roger Lanford as her attorney. She was more than a little embarrassed when Roger chuckled in response.

"Pardon my mess. Barb accuses me of being a hoarder. I do, however, know what every file is and where they all are. My filing system is… unique that's all. Your grandmother and I knew each other for years, we went to high school together in Covington." Roger Lanford was five-foot six, broad in stature, his middle thickened with age. His suit was rumpled and he walked with the hint of a limp, favoring his left leg. Gray hair floated above the crown of his head, his jowls sagged bringing his dark brown eyes with them. Tessa found she liked him immediately. Despite the mess and the disheveled appearance, he was kind. He was the antithesis of every lawyer she had ever dealt with, including herself, and that made her smile.

"I'm sorry to have embarrassed you. I had a very long drive here yesterday and I'm a little out of my element. Please forgive me," Tessa begged.

"Your grandmother hated coming here to my office, I always met with her at her – your home. She was able to overlook my disorganization because she trusted me. She always said there was no substitute for history."

"Mr. Lanford…"

"Roger, please."

"Roger, I am here to start the renunciation to excuse me from being the executor of Marian's will."

"If that's what suits you, my dear." (Did everyone in this town have to call her dear?)

"It does suit me. The quicker the better. I'd like to be on my way home to Chicago tonight if at all possible." Tess's voice was thin and tight.

"I'll just need a few signatures from you after I organize the paperwork."

Softening, Tess allowed her shoulders to relax. "Also, I would like the keys to Front Street so I can retrieve some of my Grandfather's belongings?" Tessa added by way of a question. She hadn't realized until this moment how important it felt to her that she go to Front Street and reclaim her memories of Henry.

"Sure, I have the keys right here..." Roger reached into a bottom drawer, pulled out a lock box, spun the combination and handed Tessa the keys.

"Thank you." Tess cleared her throat. "Roger, could I ask you a few questions?"

"Certainly, I'll answer if I can. What would you like to know?"

"I read Marian's obituary in the *Chapel Corners Gazette* this morning. Do you know why Marian chose the Children's Action Organization as the designated charity for donations?" Roger's brow furrowed together in a tight set of ones between his eyes.

"She came to me shortly after your twenty-first birthday and asked that I change her will to enlist you as the executor. It was then she requested CAO as the beneficiary of any donations."

"But you don't know why?"

"Not specifically, no."

"Not specifically? Or no?" Tess responded.

"Tessa, I know you were estranged from your grandmother... for a very long time. It must have been difficult for you."

"It was the first eighteen years that were difficult, Mr. Lanford." Tess's tone was more curt than she intended.

"Actually, it was really only the years after my Grandpa Henry passed away that were difficult."

"I'm sorry to hear that, although not surprised." Henry intertwined his fingers and rested them on the desk.

Tessa rose from her seat and turned to leave, eager to get to Front Street. Before walking out of Roger's office door, she turned and asked, "How did she die?"

"She had a heart attack making dinner. When she didn't come to an elder's meeting at church, they called the police to look for her. Marian was a lot of things, but unreliable was not one of them. They found her in the kitchen. I will call you when the paperwork is ready to sign."

Tess excused herself with the keys and walked out of the office. A rumble of anxiety filled her stomach as she made her way to Front Street. It was time to go home.

Chapter Eleven

The drive toward Front Street was short. Tessa kept the driver's window down and let her hand coast up and down on the wave of the wind. Lawns were small and, despite the warm weather, were still winter brown with small patches of new, tender, green grass. Most were neatly manicured (all except Mr. Barger's, his grass was already long, even for this early in the season). Daffodils and crocuses in all variety of colors sprinkled the walkways and flowerbeds. She had loved to plant bulbs in the fall with Henry. From the first thaw, Henry and Tessa would begin a vigil, waiting for the first crocuses to burst through last year's mulch, heralding summer's coming out party.

Tess parked the car and reached to the bottom of her purse to pull out her phone. She pushed down the power button, turning up the ringer so she would be sure to hear Roger's call. The phone pinged with voicemails and text messages, but Tess put it back in her purse without looking at who they were from. It was a strange sense of liberation to disconnect from her phone, at home she was physically and mentally tied to it.

There were seventeen steps from the sidewalk to the front door. It had been one thousand and thirty-six steps from her fifth-grade bus stop to the front door. That was the year the counting began, the year Henry died.

The house faced west, toward the lake. The rising sun had not yet cleared the peak of the roof. Tess was eerily calm as she walked in the shadow of her childhood home. *Fifteen, sixteen, seventeen.*

With the key in her left hand, she slipped the metal puzzle piece into its partner and turned. *Click, click, thunk, swish.* The door was silent as it opened into the entryway of the small Cape Cod. The sun poured through the dust-soaked air, casting a triangle of light onto the floor, bringing to life the colors of the Oriental rug that had been in the front foyer of her grandmother's home since Tessa was young. Magenta, fire red, orange and green — they were all faded with time, but also, oddly, exactly the same.

"Hello? Anyone home?" Tess couldn't help announcing herself.

Silence. A small ripple of relief cascaded down Tessa's back and caught on the knot that had taken up residence in her belly. The door closed behind her with a familiar thud. The stale, dry air hit her. There was still a trace of Marian here: the familiar scent of laundry starch and peas.

She turned on the light and cautiously walked farther into the house. By abruptly turning right, Tess could avoid the kitchen. Her grandfather's den was just as it had been her entire life. The walls were covered in dark paneling, with orange and brown shag carpet. His hand-crafted water filter sat in the corner right by his favorite wing backed chair. Tessa closed her eyes and took a sweeping breath in. She imagined she could still smell his pipe, the sweet, heavy scent of cherry tobacco lingering in the air. He had been gone for seventeen years and still this room, *his* room, gave Tess comfort that she hadn't realized she craved. Tess reached up and released the rolled shade to the top of the window. *Good morning, Grandpa Henry. I'm back.* The sunlight poured into the room and Tess felt defiant. She turned to the window on the next wall and threw up that shade, too. "Good morning, Grandpa Henry!" she sang. Tess twisted the lock on top of the old window, rusty and stubborn. It finally budged. Once the windows were open, beautiful birdsong flooded into the room on the back of the warm May morning breeze.

The autographed basketball from the 1960 Chapel Corners High School State Championship game was still in its case on the top of the built-in bookshelves. In all the years that Tess had lived here, the house had been a tomb. Blinds were kept shut, windows were never opened. *The Great Gatsby*, *The Catcher in the Rye*, *Little Women*, yes even *Little Women*, graced the walls of Henry Wallace's bookshelves. He was a reader, a connoisseur of the written word. Henry would more often than not fall asleep in the evening in his favorite chair, pipe in hand, one of the great classics in the other. Marian could never understand why Henry read to such excess, but Tessa did. He read to escape to a place more fruitful, more exciting, and more colorful. He read to escape the tomb.

Tessa ran her fingers along the spines of her grandfather's books. The leather-bound covers embossed with the timeless titles. Tess began to cry, gentle, sweet tears. Tess pulled a copy of *Pride and Prejudice* off the shelf and ran her hands over the cover of the book. This had been one of her grandfather's favorites. She had played for many hours at his feet while he flipped the pages of this book. It was as close to home, as close to family, as close to peace as her soul had felt since the day he left this Earth. She split the pages with her thumbs, picking a spot in the middle to open the book and began reading aloud. "I cannot fix on the hour, or the spot, or the look or the words, which laid the foundation. It is too long ago. I was in the middle before I knew that I had begun." Tess read Mr. Darcy's response to Elizabeth's question, when had he fallen in love with her?

"I was in the middle before I knew that I had begun," Tess read out loud again. "Thanks, Grandpa," Tess whispered.

Tess had been eight or nine before she asked who her father was. It wasn't with the longing or curiosity that she had for her mother. Tess had always believed that to be because Grandpa Henry filled those shoes so well. She never went without a father figure in her life. She was too young to understand the gravity of how she landed in this world with no biological parents to raise her, so Henry's explanation that her father had gone away after her mother died was comfortable and simple. He was just gone, he wasn't there. But Henry was. That was all she had ever needed. After Henry died her mind had wandered to the idea of her father from time to time. In the end, Henry was the best father and grandfather she could have asked for. She saved her craving and imaginings for Caroline, for dreaming of the mother she never had.

The house was small. A kitchen, Henry's den, and a dining area along with a small guest bathroom off of the living area made up the downstairs. Upstairs had two bedrooms, one Marian and Henry's the other Tessa's (Caroline's before that). Tessa had come to collect a few of Grandpa Henry's artifacts. She thought she would breeze in, have a look around choose a few items, sign the renunciation and head back to Chicago. She closed the book and laid it on Henry's desk. It would come back with her.

Growing up, the dining room had been covered with the same rusty shag carpet as the den. Now an antique dining table covered what looked to be the original hard wood floors, refinished. The room was small but the table was large, leaving only enough room for the tall chairs to be pulled away and used. A large wrought iron light fixture hung from the ceiling, looking as though it might pull the plaster with it like a soggy cardboard box. Marian had been given a few antiques over the years from her parents as well as her in-laws. Tess had never paid much mind, but now she wished she knew which pieces were from the Wallaces and which were from Marian's family, the Sattlers.

In the area leading from the dining room into the living space there was an antique secretary desk with a roll top. Tess had loved this piece as a child and used it to play "office" and "school." Her favorite game, though, had been to pretend to be the old-fashioned telephone operator on *Little House on the Prairie.* The show was on re-runs by the time she was old enough to watch it. She would pretend to connect phone lines and people, busying herself with hours of imaginary friends to talk to. Tessa guessed now that the piece had likely belonged to Henry's mother, because Tessa was allowed to play with it.

The carpet in the living area was replaced by a midnight blue plush and the walls were still white. A matching love seat and couch in blue-and-purple irises filled up most of the small space. Magazines were orderly, kept in a basket next to the rocking chair next to the fireplace. *Ladies Home Journal, Reader's Digest,* and *Guideposts* were filed neatly in order of date, and all had cracked spines.

On the mantle of the fireplace were two photographs. One was of Caroline when she was six years old and was the proud owner of a smile missing four teeth. She was wearing a red gingham tunic with watermelon trim, yellow shorts and small, dirty white tennis shoes. The picture's age was creeping close to Caroline's eyes, bleeding the color from the photograph. The second frame held a photograph of Grandpa Henry in his work uniform, a black jumpsuit with his name embroidered on the left pocket. His face is blurred just a bit, like he was caught talking in mid-sentence. The photos sat on the mantle during all the years that Tessa lived in this house.

Sadness crept around Tess and she pulled the picture of her mother down for a closer look. There was such fire in her mother's eyes. She was a spitfire, her spirit jumped right out of the faded photograph and buoyed Tess. Marian was strict, rules were meant to be followed and she was meant to make the rules. Children were to be seen and not heard and their needs were mere inconveniences to the Christian life she was living. Caroline would have tested Marian, they would have been oil and water.

Tess could not claim that Marian was abusive. Her basic needs were met: she was clothed, fed and had shelter and heat. She was taken to the doctor and church and school. There had been swimming lessons and a vacation or two. Marian's cool indifference to Tess, the vague neglect, shaped Tess in a way that made it hard for her to give and accept warmth. Tess was raised to believe she was a burden.

Growing up Tessa was told that Caroline had died in childbirth, that her body had started bleeding and they could not stop it. Her time had grown thin just as Tessa's had begun. She had been robbed of her mother, just as Caroline had been robbed of her life with Tessa. Tessa always saw them together, Caroline and Tess, as the victims, both mother and daughter suffering a huge loss. Losing her mother was a wound Tessa carried with her daily. Her life was built around the loss and she believed certain things about herself because of it. Tess had never considered what a loss that was for Marian and how losing her only daughter had changed her. Caroline's death had been Tess's to own, she had not left room for Marian to share the grief with her. Still, it didn't erase the last fight they had, the awful, spiteful things that Marian had hurled at her.

. . . .

Tessa hadn't meant to find it. She was working on her senior project for school, she needed something, though she can't remember the details anymore. Did she need a Sharpie? Scissors? Something. She remembered looking through the kitchen drawers and not finding it. She remembered walking into Henry's den and stopping for a second. After Henry had died, Tessa was no longer allowed in his room, but Marian wasn't home and she really needed the supplies to finish the project, so she went in anyway.

The paper was folded in quarters, tucked under the pens and pencils in Grandpa Henry's top left drawer. Caroline's name was written on the outside, and Tessa's curiosity of all things Caroline was too strong to contain. She pulled the paper out and, in one moment, everything Tessa knew to be true was destroyed.

Tessa had run screaming from Henry's den and upstairs to her bedroom, her voice was thick with trauma. The truth seeped into the crevices of her bones and pockets of air drained from her lungs. Tessa whirled herself in circles, one way then the other; she heaved a vase across the room, plunging a hole in the wall. Water seeped down the drab white paint like sap from a tree. The daisies, her favorite, lay like dead soldiers scattered on the battlefield. Empty hangers swayed in the closet where clothes had been ripped from their order. Tess lay curled on her bed with her knees tucked up to her breasts and her arms encircling her body, squeezing out every space, trying to be small.

That's where she was when Marian found her that night.

"Did you think I would never find out?" Lying in bed, facing the wall, Tessa's voice was small, barely audible.

"What are you talking about?" Marian spat back.

Tess threw the crumpled death certificate at Marian. It flew a fraction of the distance and landed on the floor. "Did you think I would never find out?" She spoke more loudly now.

"I see," Marian said, standing defiantly, refusing to pick up the paper from the floor. Bile rose in Tess's throat.

"What do you mean 'I see'? What the hell." Tessa stood. Lying still was worse than standing to face Marian.

"Do not use profanity with me, Tessa Wallace."

"What the hell does 'I see' mean? What does that mean? What? Have you just been laughing at me all these years waiting for me to find out the truth? Why didn't you just tell me? Why? *Why*?" Tessa paused, taking pointy breaths. "Why didn't you? It would have saved you a lot of grief!" She was embarrassed, ashamed. She had believed her mother loved her.

"Do you honestly think that telling you that my teenage daughter swallowed enough pills to kill a two-hundred-pound man would have saved me a lot of grief? You don't know anything about grief." Marian's face was tilted forward, her eyes drawn only to the paper on the floor as if she stared at it long enough it would change the past, change the truth that was written in black and white. "I have spent your whole life trying to shelter you from this – you just *have* to break the rules, don't you Tessa? Can't leave well enough alone. You are always walking around here like the injured party when all along I let you believe a lie to protect you. Well there you go. Now your perfect little picture of your perfect little mother is gone. She killed herself."

"What did you do to her? What did you do to her that made her swallow those pills?" Tessa picked up the paper off the floor and held it in Marian's face. "What did you do?"

"This is the thanks I get for cleaning up my daughter's mess. You can't even be grateful."

"Grateful? Grateful? What do I have to be grateful for? Let's see… you lied to me, you ignore me, you don't care if I live or die, and you hate me! I should just take a bunch of pills and go be with my mother! Anything has to be better than here!"

"Tessa Henrietta Wallace get a hold of yourself. I will not discuss this with you while you are out of control."

"You never discuss anything whether I am out of control or not. You never talk about Grandpa Henry to me… you ignore dead people about as good as you ignore me! You'd just as soon forget I exist!" Tessa pushed too far.

"I could never forget you exist. It's your fault she's gone. Do you hear me? You want to know the truth? Do you? I'll tell you the truth. She was so embarrassed that she got herself pregnant, so ashamed at having brought you into this world that she couldn't stand to be in it. That's why she took those pills! It was because of *you*. My daughter left this Earth because of your very presence in it, and I have been forced for all these years to look at your face. Every day."

Turning away from her grandmother, Tessa's hands came to her ears in a rapid attempt to block out the words that were pounding at her. The hate spilled from Marian out onto the floor, seeping up Tess like a tree drinks the rain. "No… no… no. You're lying! She didn't hate me! She loved me. She loved me more than you ever did!" Tessa pressed past her grandmother, running down the stairs, taking two at a time. Marian followed her quickly, her feet tapping on the hard wood of the steps. They reached the living room at the same time.

"Oh, really? Why else would she kill herself just three weeks after your birth? She was embarrassed. She couldn't get over how she shamed your grandfather and me."

"Don't you talk about my grandpa!"

"He was my husband. Do not tell me anything about Henry."

"He loved me." Tess's words were steadfast.

Marian's lips curled upward on the creases where her coral lipstick clumped like tacky glue. "If he loved you so much why did he lie to you?"

"He loved me." Tess repeated.

Marian's hand struck Tessa clean and hard across the right cheek. The sensation was crisp and hot, knocking

Tessa backward. Her back rolled across the wall like a rolling pin, piece-by-piece. Her neck strained to keep her head from planting itself against the hard brick of the fireplace as she stumbled sideways toward the hearth. She had never feared Marian physically, so she had not seen the strike coming.

"He loved me." She repeated through her tears. She may not have known the truth about her mother, but she damn well knew the truth about Henry. Tessa walked past her grandmother and out the front door.

Standing in the living room alone Tessa felt the ghosts of Marian, Henry and Caroline surround her. She touched her hand to her right cheek. She replaced the photo of young Caroline back on the mantle. Sweat dripped down her back. The truth of her mother's suicide had worn away at the fantasy of the mother-and-daughter-hippie-duo that had sustained Tessa through the darkest of times. Nothing was as it seemed.

Tessa's phone rang. Roger Lanford.

If Tessa had begun to soften toward Chapel Corners and her memories here, she remembered now why she left. The skillet-hot pain of knowing her mother did not choose to live in a world with Tess in it was a greater sorrow than any good memory of Henry, Sarah Beth, Lake Michigan or Castle Pharmacy could ever be. Tess felt the sting of Marian's final slap across her cheek a decade later. The truth was too dark, too heavy, too painful to carry. The only way out for Tess was to leave. She was right all those years ago. Leaving Chapel Corners and Marian was the only way for her to survive. Creating a new life, becoming Tessa Wallace of Chicago, Illinois was the only way Tess knew how to endure the greatest pain she ever knew. Her mother did not love her enough to stay. Tessa took the picture of Caroline back off of the mantle and tucked it into her purse before she silenced her phone and walked out of Front Street.

Chapter Twelve

Davis and Ryan were two hours into a quoting meeting for a brand-new development project. The senior Renfords had given their boys the reins to design and bid the company's latest project for Darling Development, Renford Construction's biggest client. The project was to be their coming out party. Parker and his younger brother Thomas were beginning to phase out, this would be their first step into retirement. The project had to be perfect. No mistakes, no oversights. Davis had been grateful for the project the last few days, it was a brilliant distraction from his failed relationship with Tess.

"Davis, Adrianna from A's Couture is here to see you?" Fran, Davis's executive assistant presented the statement as a question. "Do you have time to see her?"

"Yes, he most certainly does have time to see me." Adrianna breezed past Fran and waltzed right into Davis and Ryan's meeting. "Hey there, Dave." Adrianna plopped her ridiculously large purse on Davis's desk, covering the blueprints and spec sheets. She was wearing a butter yellow pashmina wrapped around a white, silk tank top coupled with white silk Capri pants and yellow sandals with ballerina ties. She wore white oversized sunglasses with dark lenses. Her now jet-black hair was piled high in a bouquet of curls with a few tendrils draped like ivy down the sides of her face.

"Dave?" Ryan repeated with a snicker.

"Who are you?" Adrianna asked.

"You are really going to walk in here, interrupt my meeting, call me *Dave* and ask him who he is?" For two years Davis had hidden his animosity for Adrianna from Tess. He didn't have to do that anymore. "Who are you?"

"I am your girlfriend's best friend." Adrianna squared her shoulders. "And the owner of the hottest boutique design house in Chicago. You know exactly who I am."

"Tess is not my girlfriend." Davis's voice was dry.

"She's in trouble, Dave." Adrianna looked Davis in the eye. "Davis." She conceded.

"What do you mean she's in trouble?" Ryan asked.

"Are you going to tell me who you are?" Adrianna asked again.

"What do you mean she's in trouble?" Davis asked, ignoring her question. Adrianna looked from Ryan to Davis and then back again, gauging the safety of proceeding with Ryan in the room.

"She left work yesterday in the middle of the day. She literally got up and walked out. Didn't go to her meeting with Holmes, you know that big one that took all her time for like the last month? Yeah. She didn't go."

"What do you mean she didn't go?" Ryan spoke for Davis.

"Again. Who *are* you?" This time Adrianna would not back down, slapping her hands on her hips.

"This is Ryan. My cousin," Davis answered. "Ryan, this is Adrianna. A friend of Tess's."

"Cousin. Best friend. Business partner. I cover all the bases." Ryan reached a hand out to shake Adrianna's. Adrianna lifted her hand for him to kiss it by way of greeting. Davis groaned.

"Seriously, Adri cut the crap. How do you know she's in trouble? Have you spoken to her?"

"No, she won't answer my calls." Adrianna was contrite in response.

"I don't see that as a problem," Davis said. "I would say that's progress." The snipe was lost on Adrianna as she rummaged through her purse looking for her phone.

"Have you spoken to her?" Adrianna asked.

"No…"

"Have you called her?" Ryan countered, looking at Davis. After their heart-to-heart on Sunday, Davis had not said a word about Tess. Ryan had taken that to mean he didn't want to talk about it and hadn't pressed him.

"I called her twice. She hasn't called me back. I haven't talked to her since Saturday night after the benefit." Davis addressed Ryan, ignoring Adrianna.

"I called Lucy. Normally she's a complete bitch to me, but she's totally worried, like I am. Like you *should be*. Tess hasn't checked in at work other than one quick text to Lucy saying she'd be back to work today."

"She isn't back?" Davis asked, his pulse quickening. He looked at his watch. 3:47.

"No. I called Lucy before I came here. She didn't come to work and didn't call in. At all," Adrianna whined. "Something is really wrong, Davis. I'm serious."

"You know she's a private person. Maybe she just

needed to be alone," Davis reasoned. Ryan watched his cousin closely.

"In a million years Tessa Wallace would never, ever skip a meeting with Holmes. Not an important one. Not one that was part of her Ten-Year Plan. Not one that could affect her making partner!" Adrianna's voice had morphed from the confident, business woman she had tried to present when she walked in to the shrill, high pitched whine she had perfected.

Davis looked down at the blueprints and spec sheets on his conference table. Had he missed something? Was Tess in trouble? Was he letting his ego get in the way of seeing the truth? He glanced up at Ryan, and his eyes told him to consider what Adrianna was saying.

"Adrianna, I haven't talked to her since after the banquet because she left my brownstone in the middle of the night. No goodbye, no text, no phone call. Not even an old-fashioned note. Nothing. And she hasn't answered my call." Davis's ego still had his heart as a strong hold. "I don't know what you want me to do about this. How am I supposed to help when she won't answer me?" Davis's conviction that he was right to walk away gained back its strength with every word. After his Day Load with Ryan and Gretchen, and the run the next day, Davis had decided to set aside his pride and call Tess. He would reach out to her, he would be the best version of his father as he could muster. He would tell her whatever she was hiding, he could help. He would support her, she would give in, let him hear her secrets and take them back to where they were on Saturday night. He would fix everything.

At first he had been disappointed that she hadn't answered. He hadn't left a message out of spite. If she couldn't be bothered to pick up the phone, he couldn't be bothered to leave a message. Later that night over a Goose and soda alone in his brownstone he realized that not leaving the message was a mistake. Maybe she needed to hear his voice. So he had called again this morning. Still nothing. Davis wasn't accustomed to being dismissed and ignored. His ego was winning the war over Tess's heart today. If Tess wanted to fix this, she would have to come to him. He was done putting himself in harm's way.

"I don't know why she does what she does, Davis. I really don't. But I have known Tessa for a lot longer than you and I am telling you something is wrong. Period. You can believe me or not, but I am right." Adrianna tacked back toward the professional. It was then Davis realized that Adrianna was not nearly as shallow or as stupid as he had taken her to be. Her persona was just that, a manufactured brand. There was a lot more to Adrianna from A's Couture than Davis had given her credit for.

"What do you want me to do, Adri?" Davis used Tess's nick name for her friend.

"I want you to fix this!" Adrianna began to cry. "I feel it in my bones. I'm telling you. Something is wrong. She may not be answering, but she needs us. She needs you."

"Do you have any idea where she might be?" Ryan brokered trust between the two adversaries.

"She grew up in Michigan. She didn't have much family, her mother died when was young. She literally spent every holiday, break and long weekend in college with me and my crazy-ass family. So you know she had nowhere else to go." Adrianna smirked, wiping the tears from her perfectly lined eyes.

Davis was taken aback. He had no idea she had grown up in Michigan. He knew her parents were gone, but he knew nothing more. Adrianna and Tess's friendship began to make more sense. As much of a dingbat as Adrianna was, there was a low-level surveillance always paying attention. If Davis decided to go after Tess, to try and find her and help her, he would need Adrianna's help. Davis swallowed hard, deciding to make a deal with the devil.

"I'll try to call her again." Davis picked up his phone and dialed her number. He hung up before the call connected. What the hell would he say to her? What would he say while Ryan and Adrianna stood waiting? No, calling her again won't work. Adri had tried. He had tried. Lucy had tried.

Lucy. Lucy was the only one Tess had responded to. He would have to start there.

"I have an idea." Davis tucked his phone into his back pocket. "Ry…"

"I got it buddy, I'll finish up for today. You go." Ryan stood, patting Davis on the back.

"All right, Adrianna. You win. Let's go." Adrianna grabbed her ridiculously big purse off of the blueprints and spec sheets and smiled at Ryan as she followed Davis out the door.

Chapter Thirteen

Tessa walked the nine blocks from Front Street back toward the Waterside Inn and the path to the lake, counting her steps to one hundred and then beginning again. She was hungry, tired and wearing the same clothes she had put on yesterday morning in Chicago before she left her apartment. After two blocks the shoes were gone, tucked into her purse next to the framed photo of Caroline. The sun was deep in the afternoon sky. She had spent longer than she planned at Front Street, and had left with only her mother's picture. Her thoughts were fragmented, shooting around inside her head like darts missing their mark.

Tess passed the hotel and headed down the path that led to the lake. Her feet, sore from the cobbled sidewalks and gravel-sprinkled roads were welcomed by the soft sand. The canopy of trees greeted her, her breath pulled in and out slowly. She made it to the opening, plopped her purse on the sand and then her body. Tessa contemplated the massive body of water in her view.

Lake Michigan had anchored her as a little girl and then a young woman, the heaviness of the water held her to this Earth, connected her to her mother and after Henry's death, it connected her to him as well. Growing up with Marian had been trying, but mostly lonely, and

Tessa had company with the moon here at the beach. After Henry died, when Marian retired to her room, Tessa would sneak out of her second story window, shimmy down the television antennae and walk the nine blocks to the water. She found consolation in the churning of the waves, the constant energy of the water and the absolute predictability of the lake. The beach changed as the seasons did. As days and weeks and months wove in and out of each other, the landscape of the sand would grow fuller in some places, thin in others — but the water was always steadfast.

Many nights Tess only read, first Judy Bloom and Laura Ingalls Wilder, and then Yeats and Frost became her favorites. She read *Pride and Prejudice* on this beach. When it was warm enough, Tess would swim under the light of the moon and stars. It was always brighter here against the inky expanse of the water's horizon. On the nights she swam, she would walk straight away to the water's edge, keeping one foot in front of the other until she was nearly submerged. There she would find her release. Her muscles would go limp, her mind would be cleared and her body would float into the water like blueberries in a pancake. Tess loved the silent refuge the water provided. She would stay under as long as she could. Leaving her control limp, she would turn and sway with the will of the water. Coming up only briefly for air, she would go under again, returning to the place where the voices in her head were quiet, where no one had left her and she was free of the consuming loneliness.

Tonight the water was cold, her toes felt the painful

prick first. Burning and numbness came quickly, creeping up her bare legs toward the hem of her skirt. Tessa pressed on through the frigid water. Pieces of memories floated in and around her: her turquoise ring, ice cream at Castle's, Caroline's tall trees, Jaco Beach, lemon cheesecake, apple trees, *Chapel Corners Gazette,* Marian's will, Roger Lanford, the shark tank, Henry... Davis. The water reached her waist, and the burning numbness of the water was welcome. She preferred the physical pain to the pain her heart felt from losing Henry, losing Caroline. She sunk into the silky stillness of the water, held gingerly from hitting bottom by the weight of the water. The weight of her sins, of her past, of her memories held her under.

Caroline's suicide had become part of Tess's DNA, she replicated the story with every breath. Caroline's story became hers. She came to believe that she was little more than the grown child of a mother who didn't love her. Believing your mother didn't love you changes who you are, changes how you see yourself in the world around you. Tessa danced underwater, the churning and spilling of the waves directing her. Her body was weightless, her mind still. It had always been here, in the water, where she felt centered. She had long since questioned her religion and the fairness of God in this world, but here, in this grand expanse of nature she felt part of a spiritual world. The water gave her a connection to life that she could not find on the streets of Chicago, in the board room at CH&E, at the CAO benefit, on Front Street or with Davis in his brownstone. Because under the water,

Tessa was stripped down to the truth. There are no lies, no stories, no cover ups and no hiding. Tessa was real. More memories came, Marian packing her lunch, Marian driving her to school, Marian buying her school clothes, Marian folding her laundry, Marian making dinner. Marian had never been warm, she had never nurtured or coddled Tessa, but she did care for her. Grief swept through Tessa with every new wave. Caroline, Henry and Marian.

Peace came to Tess in a quiet motionlessness, wrapping her with comfort, making her believe she was the gill-breathing little girl of her dreams. The pain of the May water felt good backed up against the pain of her grief. The stillness was where her peace came. Her lungs burning, she lay dormant. The cold, the grief, the confusion, the pain was all too heavy for Tessa to lift herself from the water. She waited for the desire to breathe to win against the weight of the water and the desire to be still. Nothing came. Tessa wearing her Mary Jane's, Caroline in her gingham tunic with watermelon trim, apples hanging from branches against the sky, strawberry milkshakes, Jaco Beach, Davis… Davis.

Arms wrapped around her waist, sucking her from the icy water. Her lungs burned with the air she gasped. "I've got you, I've got you." The man whispered as he lifted her up above the surface. Water fell away from her clothes, dripped from her body, with it the stillness and peace of surrendering. *No!* she thought. *Put me back, please just put me back.* The sun warmed her skin, her lungs heaved air in and out, desperate to catch up. The man was running. The canopy of pines on the path to the Waterside cast shadows of light and dark across them both as he ran.

Tess heard him scream, "Help me! I need blankets, she needs to get warm!"

"Oh dear, oh Tessa! Oh honey, what did you do?" She felt Reenie's warm hand on her forehead. *I didn't mean to!* Tessa cried out in her mind. *I didn't mean to, I just want it to stop hurting. I just don't want to hurt anymore.* Tessa felt the man and Reenie move quickly around her as she shivered violently. Tessa tried to speak, but her words would not come. "Put her here, right on the couch. I'll get hot water bottles, and I have a heating blanket," she heard Reenie direct the man.

Blankets piled on Tess while she continued to shiver. Warm bottles of water were tucked under them against her skin. No concept of time, Tessa continued to shiver. She felt Reenie and the man fussing over her, adding blankets, changing out wet ones. The shivering and heat began to revive her, her eyes struggled open. "I'm so sorry, Reenie. I'm sorry. I didn't mean to," Tess whispered. Her voice felt thick, her words dense.

"Oh sweetheart. Are you ok?" Reenie turned to look behind her. "She's awake now! She's awake." Tess looked around, looking for the man who saved her. Reenie turned back to Tessa, maternal comfort oozing over Tessa like honey on a biscuit.

"I'm ok. I am. I'm ok. Just really, really cold still."

"Tessa. It's nice to see you with your eyes open." A man with a gentle smile and sandy blonde hair leaned down on one knee next to Tess.

"It's you," Tess said. A quiet look passed between Reenie and the man.

"It's who, honey?" Reenie questioned.

"The man from the beach. You're the runner from this morning. I saw you on the beach this morning after I did yoga. And again at the coffee shop…" Tessa said.

"That was me. I ran this morning and was taking a quick walk on the beach before I headed home, taking advantage of the warm weather. I'm Luke, Tessa. Luke Castle. I knew you as a little girl."

"Castle Pharmacy!" Tessa's eyes sparked thru their haze. "My Grandpa Henry took me to get ice cream there all the time. Thank you so much for getting me out of the water. I guess I didn't realize how cold it was." Tessa's teeth chattered, her eyes fluttered shut like a butterfly resting her wings. "I didn't mean to drown. I really didn't. I just wanted… I just wanted to be in the water." Tess's voice thinned to a whisper.

"Your Grandpa Henry did bring you in. Every week," Luke Castle answered Tessa. "I'm going to let you get some rest. Reenie, do you need me anymore?"

"No, dear, no. Tessa and I can get her to her room. I'll help her into a warm bath."

"I'm going to head home and get some warm clothes on, too." Luke smiled.

"Oh my goodness! I am so sorry, Mr. Castle. I didn't even notice you are soaked. I am so sorry."

"No worries, kiddo. None at all. You get warmed up. And please, call me Luke."

Tessa smiled. "Thank you, Luke."

Luke addressed Reenie, "You call me if you need anything. If she doesn't stop shivering and warm up pretty quickly, she needs to go to ER. If that's the case, please call me."

"Got it. We will get her warmed up and tucked in bed." Reenie smiled at Tessa. "I'll be right back, dear. I'm going to walk Luke out."

"Thank you so much, Luke. I feel so foolish. Thank you."

Luke smiled at Tessa. He reached his hand out toward Tessa's forehead, his hand hung suspended for a splash of time before he pulled it back and walked away.

Tessa closed her eyes and let the warmth of the cocoon Reenie and Luke had built her protect her from the fear of what had almost happened. Tessa hadn't wanted to die, she had only wanted to lay down the yoke of grief and pain that she had been carrying all her life. In the silence of the lobby of the Waterside Inn, Tessa lay on the blue 1970s davenport and realized what she needed to do. It was time to stop running.

....

"So, Reenie... what's up with the purple scarves?" Reenie warmed up chicken noodle soup and homemade bread for them both. Tessa devoured hers and asked for seconds. Reenie had refused to leave Tessa in her room alone for the evening, so the new friends watched the Gameshow Channel and Reenie knitted while Tessa continued to warm up.

"Most people don't ask. Most people just assume I've lost my ability to accessorize!" Reenie laughed. She took a deep breath before she continued. "I was married to Harvey for fifty-one years. We had the boys, Clay and Charlie. They are all grown now. I can't complain, Harvey was a good man, kind and he provided well. It was a good life. It just wasn't mine." Reenie paused, shrugging both shoulders and looking out the window in the direction of the great lake. Tess wiped her mouth with her napkin and placed it carefully on her lap. "Harvey didn't want me to work. He wanted me to be home with Clay and Charlie. So I stayed. I gave up my dreams to stay home and be a mother. I'm not saying I would have traded the boys or my time with them, God knows I love them to pieces; but given the chance I would have worked."

"What would you have done?"

"I wanted to be a writer, for the paper. A journalist. I had a degree from Michigan State in English. I wanted a purpose; I wanted to use my mind. I cooked, I cleaned, and washed clothes and I ironed. Again, I would not have traded my time with my boys, I always felt I would have been more than I was — a better mother — if I had had something of my own." Reenie was wistful.

"What does that have to do with purple scarves?" Tessa asked gently.

"Hmm…" Reenie smiled at Tessa. "When Harvey died, I was lost. I had spent so many years letting him make all the choices I didn't know what to do with the rest of my life. I was really lost. The boys were all grown up, and my husband was gone. I had no idea who I was or what I was meant to do after. You know *after* my life's work was over. I spent months at home alone. Cleaning, cooking too much food for one person, ironing Harvey's shirts even though he was gone. Clay lives in San Francisco and Charlie lives in Dallas, and after their dad died they had to go back to their lives. That was the point of all my work being their momma, for them to move on and have their own lives. They call me and text me! I learned how to text. I even know how to FaceTime! But I had too much time alone. So, one day I got up, got dressed and got a job. That was here at the Waterside. Harvey had enough money saved that I don't need the income, but I need *the reason*. I spend every hour I can here, and I write. I write down what I see on Superior Avenue, I write about the customers we have here, I write stories about the people I meet and about the conversations I hear. It makes me happy." Reenie smiled, still working her needles back and forth.

"Reenie, I still don't get the purple scarf thing," Tessa questioned, laughing in return.

"Harvey hated purple. He never wanted me to wear it and it has always been my favorite color. Soon after I started working here I went shopping in Covington at the Green Apple. It's the cutest little boutique! I found my first purple scarf, bought it with the money I had earned on my own. I put it on right there in the store. I'd bought it with my own money, it was my favorite color, and I wore it to my own job. It pleased me so much that now I always wear a purple scarf." Reenie shrugged her shoulders. "Reminds me to make my own choices. And besides, purple is still my favorite color!"

"I wanted to be a writer, too. I went to Northwestern, my undergrad degree is in English," Tess confessed.

"Really, dear? Well then how did you end up in law school?"

"I don't know. I guess I thought writing wouldn't be enough. I wanted certain success more than I wanted to write, maybe?"

"Don't you think you could have been successful at writing?"

"At the time I didn't." Tess was quiet. She laid back and pulled the covers up tight under her chin.

"I supposed that would depend on your definition of success, wouldn't it?" Reenie continued to knit, furiously linking loose yarn into a web, creating the beginning of a pattern.

Tessa sat quietly. *Definition of success.* "I like purple, too," Tessa smiled. "Reenie, have you written any stories about me since I got here?"

"No, dear." Reenie looked into Tessa's green eyes. "You need to write your own story."

Chapter Fourteen

Davis was accustomed to people noticing him. Walking into CH&E he was on a mission, he garnered more attention than usual.

"Lucy, Davis Renford. I need to speak with you." Davis breezed right past Lucy opened Tessa's office door and waltzed in turning on the light. Adrianna followed behind Davis.

"Mr. Renford…"

"Please, call me Davis."

"Actually, he prefers Dave." Adrianna smirked, throwing her purse down on Tess's desk.

"Davis, what can I do for you?" Lucy ignored Adrianna.

"Do you know where Tess is?" Davis wasted no time. "Neither Adrianna nor I have had any luck getting ahold of her since she left."

"Davis, I don't know where she is. I really don't. I am just as confused by all of this as you are." Lucy had been increasingly worried about her boss since Tessa's disappearance on Monday morning. She had called Tessa and she had received a brief text in response, but nothing since. Lucy was fond of Tess, she admired her tenacity. She was tough and intelligent, and no one in the practice worked harder. "I have been her assistant for three years and she has never missed a day of work. Not one. I am fielding calls from Drew Libbey, Stan Epstein and others on the Hartford case. She had a huge meeting scheduled for Monday afternoon with Holmes. She had been prepping for several weeks, we talked about it when she came in Monday morning, everything was prepped and ready to go. I was away from my desk for a few minutes, came back and she was leaving. She said she would check in, and she did yesterday. I haven't heard a word from her today."

"You didn't think to ask her where she was going?" Adrianna accused. She stood next to Davis, enjoying the interrogation. Adrianna may have had more depth than Davis had first suspected, but she was still a drama queen. As worried as she was about Tess, she was equally excited about the drama.

"Of course I did. She was white as a sheet, she wouldn't tell me anything. I am really concerned," Lucy answered.

"Did something happen before she left? Did she say she was ill? Was she having trouble with anyone here at the firm that would have upset her?" The idea didn't feel plausible at all, but Davis had to ask.

"She came in drinking her regular chai latte. She spilled a little."

"Of course she did." Adrianna began to cry. "She was such a klutz sometimes." Davis turned his gaze squarely at Adrianna. Obviously, Adrianna was right, something was up with Tess. Still, he wasn't convinced she was in as much trouble as Adrianna was insisting, but he wasn't willing to ignore Adrianna's crazy instincts either.

"Anything else happen before she left, Lucy?"

"She got a phone call right before she left. When I was away from my desk, she must have answered the line herself. She was distracted after the call, she told me she had some things she had to take care of and she would check in with me later." Lucy twisted her hands together as she spoke. "I asked if I could help, if she needed anything. She said no and left."

"You picked a great time to not be at your desk, Luce." Adrianna shot at Lucy.

"Adrianna." Davis reprimanded her with a glance. "Lucy, do you think the caller would have called the main switchboard first or did they call her direct line? Maybe Theresa knows who she spoke to." She might have run out on him on Sunday morning, but Tessa would never run out on Charles Holmes. Chadwick, Holmes and Epstein was her life's ambition, she would not jeopardize her career for anything. Tiny beads of perspiration were beginning to form on his brow. Davis had thought that if he gathered Adrianna, Lucy and himself in one room they would have the information needed to find Tess, or at least ensure her safety. It had become apparent to Davis how secluded Tess had become, how disconnected she was from the people who cared about her. For a woman so widely admired for both her talents and her beauty, her pool of friends was surprisingly shallow.

Somehow her lack of meaningful attachments comforted Davis. He thought back to Saturday night when he and Tessa had made love. They had connected, he was sure of it. She had let him in where he was certain no one else had been. He pushed hard against his doubt to believe that she needed him now.

"Roger Lanford." Adrianna's voice was full of smug conviction as she spun herself in circles in Tessa's chair. She did know her best friend! She had only to think about what Tessa would have done and she figured it out. "Roger Lanford from Chapel Corners."

"Chapel Corners?" Lucy questioned.

"What are you talking about, Adri?" Davis asked.

"If I were Tess and I answered the phone, I would have been sitting here in my chair. She doodles. She always doodles. Here, she wrote it here on this pad of paper."

"Lucy, do you know who Roger Lanford is? Does he have anything to do with CH&E?"

"Davis!" Adrianna shot back. "When I was helping Tess get ready before the benefit on Saturday she got a call from Chapel Corners, Michigan. She asked me to check her phone in case it was you and it was an unidentified caller from Chapel Corners. I assumed it was a robo call and sent it to voicemail."

"Saturday?" Davis asked.

"Yes, Saturday before the gala," Adrianna answered.

"I'll make a few calls, give me a minute." Lucy stepped to her desk leaving Adrianna and Davis alone.

"You believe me now, don't you, Dave?"

"Something's up. She might run out on me, but you are right, she would never run out on work." Davis tapped his fingers on Tess's desk.

"Maybe we should let her be. Maybe she needs her space. She is never one to show her cards. Maybe we should respect that." Adrianna hedged her bets, afraid her affinity for drama had lead her down this path. Suddenly Adrianna felt protective of Tess's privacy.

"No."

"Is that for your sake or hers, Davis?"

"Both."

Lucy walked back into Tess's office, offering a paper to Davis. "I spoke with Theresa at the main switchboard and she said that she isn't aware of a Roger Lanford that Tessa would have had dealings with here at CH&E. So, I Googled him. Roger Lanford is listed as the sole lawyer at Lanford and Associates in Chapel Corners, Michigan. I have a cousin who works at a shipyard up there. I've actually been to Chapel Corners. It's a fairly small town just outside of Covington, Michigan. I don't know if Tessa is there, but here's Lanford's number."

"Thank you, Lucy. Thank you very much." Davis walked out of Tess's office with Roger Lanford's number and a decision. Adrianna was right, something was up with Tessa, but she was also right that Tessa valued her privacy. Valued it enough to walk away from Davis, Adrianna, Lucy, CH&E and her meeting with Holmes. Davis could never live with that. He needed intimacy, he needed honesty and he needed to be needed. He would find Tess. He would find her and make sure she was safe, and then he would let her go.

. . . .

Davis ran up the steps to Renford Construction two at a time. Roger Lanford's phone number was tucked safely in his pocket. He had been certain when he left Tess's office that he would head to his brownstone, make a few phone calls, find Tess and make sure she was safe. Their relationship would be final, the loose ends tied up. Instead, he found himself searching for his father. Parker was in his office on the third floor of the Renford building. The building itself was simple in design. Clean lines, and sleek, black leather furniture with chrome accents made it the opposite of CH&E's latte-inspired sanctuary. The building was built for construction; everything was durable, angled and masculine. Davis opened the door to his father's office as he knocked.

"Hey, Dad. Do you have a minute?"

"I have just a minute. I'm headed out to dinner with your mother. What do you need, Son? How was your meeting with Ryan on the Darling bid?" Parker continued straightening the piles on his glass topped desk. He adjusted his belt around his waist and smoothed his blue silk tie down with his right hand.

"I can't find Tess."

"What do you mean you can't find Tess?" Parker's face showed real concern. He had a true affection for his only son's girlfriend.

"I mean I can't find her. She left work on Monday after what I think was an unusual, if not upsetting, phone call and she hasn't been back. She won't answer my phone calls, or Adrianna's. She hasn't checked in with Lucy, her assistant, since yesterday afternoon, or with

Holmes. At all."

"Didn't she have a big meeting with Holmes this week? She told me about it at the gala."

"She didn't go," Davis answered. His leg tapping up and down.

"She didn't go? That's unlike her. Do you know who called her?"

"She wouldn't have missed that meeting for no reason. We think it may have been a lawyer in Michigan." Davis continued to fill his father in on the details of what he, Adrianna and Lucy knew about Tess's departure. Parker had returned to his seat behind his desk and was listening in earnest to what Davis had to say. He could read the signals his son was sending easily. Davis was in love with this woman. Parker had always enjoyed Tessa, they had a playful banter that blended easily into a solid working relationship when it came to business. She was an intelligent, cunning lawyer and he had admired her for that. His son's relationship with her had blossomed, and he had been certain before today that Davis had real feelings for this woman. Tess's intentions were less clear.

"What do you want to do, Son?"

"I don't know. She's a private person. Do I risk pushing her away completely by following her to some small town in Michigan based on a hunch?"

"Hasn't she already pushed herself away?" Parker asked.

Davis nodded quietly. "She's like a skittish kitten. Something scared her and she ran up a tree and I don't know if she'll ever come down."

"Hmmm…" Parker took off his glasses and pinched the bridge of his nose. Alma was so much better at these conversations. Parker and Davis had always been close, but he had handled the life skills not the emotional ones. Changing the oil, mowing a perfectly straight line in the lawn, opening doors for elders and women. He'd taught his son to read a blueprint and follow directions. Relationships were Alma's department. What would she say to their only son? Parker looked his son in the eye and took a deep breath. "Will that be enough?"

"Will what be enough?" Davis asked.

"Will it be enough to watch her high in the tree while you're here on the ground?"

"I don't follow."

Parker took another deep breath. Suddenly, he knew exactly what his wife would say. "Your mother and I lost a baby before we had you. She was in her fourth month and it devastated both of us. Your mom turned so far inside herself she pushed away your grandmother, your Aunt Lillian and me. All of us. She was convinced that no one could understand, that she was so alone in her pain that no one could share it with her."

"I never knew that." Davis's voice was respectful, quiet.

"Listen… I had to follow her up the tree. She was in so deep she couldn't figure out how to climb down. So, I either had to watch her from a different place, or go to her, be with her, hurt with her. I followed her."

"Are you telling me to track her down?"

"I'm not telling you anything. I'm telling you to

decide what will be enough. You have good instincts. You have some good information. And you have to decide if you're willing to live with her in the tree while you're on the ground or if you will go to her and help her find her way."

"What if she doesn't let me in?"

"Then you have no unanswered questions. You know you did all you could do. There's no guarantee, she may not let you in. But it seems to me, and I think to you, she's hiding something, something she's afraid of. Maybe something she's embarrassed of? What if you don't like what you learn? Will you still love her the same? There's a lot of uncertainty. So, you decide. Do you go to her, or let her go."

"Thanks a lot, Dad." Davis chuckled. He understood what Parker was telling him, but it didn't make it any easier to figure out what to do. "You've made this clear as mud."

"It's really not that difficult. What can you live with? What gives you no regrets? Will you regret not trying to find her? Or will you regret going to her? It's not so much about her as it is about you. What can you, Davis Renford, live with? What can you live without? Which decision makes you the man you want to be? With or without Tessa Wallace." Parker stood, satisfied that he would have made his wife proud. He would have to tell her over dinner. "I can call your mom and cancel, or you can join us, but either way I need to let her know. Your mom hates it when I'm late."

"Sorry, you can blame it on me. You go ahead, I've

got somethings I need to think about. Obviously."

"Oh, I intend to. The only excuse that ever gets me out of trouble with that woman is you. Listen… let me know what you decide to do."

"I'll call you." Parker patted his son on the shoulder as he moved toward the door. Davis reached in his pocket and pulled out Roger Lanford's number. Feeling the smooth paper under his fingers, he turned it around and around. What could he live with? What could he live without?

Chapter Fifteen

Reenie finally left Tessa's room around 8:00 p.m. Tessa had taken a warm bath, eaten a good meal and promised Reenie she would call if she needed her. Tessa was embarrassed that she had needed help at all, that she had stayed too long in the cold water, that she had allowed the heaviness of the past drag her under. If she was honest, she would say that Reenie's showering of attention had warmed more than her body. Her soul soaked up Reenie's nurturing care, settling into her dark corners and filling nooks that had become used to being alone.

Tessa returned Roger Lanford's phone call from earlier in the day. She left a message telling him she was going to take a few days and clean out the house and would hold off on removing herself as executor of Marian's estate until the house was finished and she had taken what she needed. She smiled knowing Roger would be pleased at her subtle change in heart.

Tessa also returned Davis's phone call, dialing his work number well after 8:00 p.m. knowing he wouldn't be there. She left him a brief message, in as strong a voice as she could muster. She told him she was away from the office and would call him when she got back to Chicago. She had wanted to add, "I will explain everything when I get home." But she hadn't. When she hung up the phone after leaving the message, she was disappointed. She had hoped he would answer.

With Reenie gone and Tessa feeling better, she became restless. Tomorrow she was going to clean out Front Street, and she needed clothes. Yoga pants that had been tucked in a corner of her gym bag and the shirt she had worn to bed last night (and to the gym last week) were not going to do it. She drove up to Covington along the cost, coveting the glimpses of the water by moonlight as she drove. Sometimes she even slowed down to soak in the view safely. How had she been living in Chicago, next to this same body of water for the last decade, and not felt its pull?

Tessa stopped at a twenty-four-hour Meijer and grabbed a few supplies: underwear, socks, flip-flops and a sweatshirt. She also grabbed a box of garbage bags, three plastic totes to pack Henry's things, a can of Pringles and a few Diet Cokes. She rounded out her purchase with a hair brush, Suave shampoo and conditioner, along with eyeliner, mascara and some blush, two lipsticks and some nail polish named Maui Waui, a pair of jeans and two cute cap sleeved T-shirts (she didn't buy the one that said "Fashionista" although she considered just for the look on Adrianna's face).

Not ready to sleep, despite the late hour, Tess took a tour of Covington on her trek back to Chapel Corners. Darkness had wrapped the town in a thick blanket, the moon had disappeared, and the clouds were thick as cotton in the sky without a crack in their façade. The shipyards looked intimidating with two large freighters alongside the dock; the equipment loomed in the night like giant steel dinosaurs. Tessa remembered coming here once or twice with Henry. He had loved his job, loved the lake and the power it had to hold such enormous ships. Having spent so much time trying to hide her past, Tess was amazed at how comfortable she was, sitting in the dark watching the silent shipyard where Henry had made his living.

Covington's Main Street was lined with grand homes, giant oaks and maples flanking the driveways at attention. They were enormous structures for private homes, most the color of candy dipped in pinks, blues and sea greens with gingerbread fixings on the eaves and wraparound porches with white picket fences around their perfectly manicured lawns. Tess thought they looked like wedding cakes, perfect places to live. As she drove slowly down Main Street toward the water, she looked up at the houses with a new curiosity. Tonight darkness hid the confection of the houses; the colors were muted tones of gray and white. Light escaped the houses from the windows creating portals into their secret lives, and Tess began watching people inside their ordinary evenings.

In the large colonial on the corner Tess glimpsed a young mother trying to comfort a crying baby alone. She bounced her on her shoulder, swaddled in a pink blanket, concern spread across the mother's face. In the Cape Cod across the street, an old man sat in his corner chair holding the newspaper by the additional light of a reading lamp, his glasses slumped down his nose, his chest rising and falling with sleep. Through another window, Tess saw a man maybe ten years her senior, working at a desk, intently staring at a computer screen while a young boy played video games upstairs in his bed.

What would someone have seen had they driven past Front Street twenty years ago? Marian would have been standing at the kitchen sink, washing the dinner dishes, lips pursed, concentration spun across her forehead. Henry would have been sitting in his den, pipe dragging from his bottom lip, a small shoelace of smoke coiled up delicately over his glasses, eyes woven together as he read. Tessa would have been writing in her diary upstairs, curled in the corner of her bed, wrapped in her lavender blanket. The lavender blanket Marian had bought for her when she had complained of being cold. A heavy sigh fell in the air. She saw things differently now. The last fight with Marian had left scars. Scars so deep Tess knew they would never heal. But that wasn't the totality of her relationship with Marian. It was complex, for certain. Rectifying the neglect and loneliness with a full belly and a warm blanket was not as difficult as she had once believed.

Tessa had held on to a narrative about Marian. For more than a decade she saw Marian's behavior as neglectful, cruel, and full of revenge for hurts Tessa had no part in. Accepting Marian where she was, remembering that Caroline did not belong to Henry and Tessa alone, was easier from a distance. Easier with Marian gone. As a young girl she had believed the impossible, that her mother would come and save her, warm her from the isolation that was her childhood.

Tessa had held Caroline over Marian's head, she had prided herself on the perfect version of her mother in direct comparison to the job Marian did every day because of Caroline's absence. Marian had taken Tess in, cared for her and met her needs. She may not have been as kind or loving as Tessa needed or wanted, but Marian's great gift was to have kept the truth of Caroline's death from her. She had tried to protect her granddaughter from the crushing pain and grief that Caroline's suicide had dominated Marian with all these years. That took all that she had to give.

Back in Chapel Corners at the Waterside Inn, Tessa drank the Diet Coke and munched on the Pringles from Meijer. The TV played an old episode of *Friends*, the strange sounds of familiar voices cut in with tracked applause made Tessa tired, exhausted even. Outside rain burst from the low hanging clouds, creating a kaleidoscope on the window as she strained to see around the corner and spot the lake. She would leave the curtains open tonight.

Sleep came easily to Tess, her body weary from the cold water, her spirit bruised from the memories. But what came easily would not last. Soon Tess was tossing and turning as her mind conjured bizarre dreams. Caught in the cobwebs of a cloudy space, Marian, Henry, Tess and Caroline held hands, their footfalls landing nowhere but leading them in a circle. Caroline was wearing the outfit she wore in the picture that was now tucked away in Tess's purse, a red gingham tunic with watermelon trim, yellow shorts and small, dirty white tennis shoes.

Henry stood as he had the last time Tess had seen him, in his dark blue grease-stained work coveralls with "Henry" embroidered in red inside a white oval on his chest. Marian was a face, the face of the obituary picture Tessa had seen just that morning, strong jaw, tight lips and gray streaks bleeding into her bland brown hair pulled tightly into a bun. The dream played from Tess's perspective, she could only see her hands, holding both Henry and Marian's, and her feet. Her feet were little, maybe seven or eight-year-old feet, and she was wearing the same dirty white tennis shoes Caroline wore. The four of them walked in a circle singing "*ring-a-round the rosie, pockets full of posies, ashes, ashes we all fall down.*" They sang the nursery song over and over until Tess's grasp on her grandparents eased, allowing Henry and Marian to float away, their bodies becoming smaller and smaller until they were no bigger than a speck of dust. Caroline stopped when the song was over and stared at Tess, smiling with her six-year-old toothless smile and the eyes of a grown woman. She smiled that way until she faded away into the cobwebs of the cloud they were suspended in.

Tessa was all alone.

Chapter Sixteen

Tess rose early and left the Waterside under a cloak of darkness from the storms, unsettled from the dreams of the night before. Pools of light came off from Main Street's new street lights, giving the downtown a charming glow. She drove through town, heading north away from the lights until they were a distant shimmer. Twists and turns in the road led Tess's Volvo deeper into the darkness, away from town, disorienting her slightly. She knew that the road she was looking for was somewhere to the east, toward the lake.

The rain showers from the night before dwindled to sprinkles. She wicked away the rain with her wipers, careful to judge the wet slickness of the road, adjusting her speed with each curve. Her turn came up quickly. With the signs of life from town long faded and the clouds covering the moon's light, she nearly missed it. The road was narrow, leading back toward a small church that was hidden in the woods near the lake. Tessa parked her car in the lot in front of the church, keeping her headlights on and pointed in the opposite direction as the building. When she turned off the engine the rush of the waves was a faint roll; the sound both comforted Tess and made her sad.

Purple darkness surrounded her, cloaking her in a

feeling of heaviness and protection. She used her phone's flashlight to navigate her steps in the darkness. The path led off of the parking lot through a white picket fence where Tessa entered the yard through a gate that was twisted off its hinges with age. Remains of spring's first crocuses wilted in the damp grass while summer yellow daffodils bloomed behind them, lining the fence. Old oak trees filled the cemetery, creating a canopy with their broad branches. The trees had hidden the earth here from the sun and Tess could feel the cold left over from winter's snow rising from the soggy dirt and grass. Gently the breeze from the lake sifted through the trees and touched Tess's face with a whisper. A moon-like glow from the flashlight followed her footsteps farther up a gentle hill, continuing on the path until she came to the spot.

HENRY WALLACE

1942-2000

LOVING FATHER, LOVING HUSBAND

Tessa ran her hands along the wet marble, tracing the lines of the etched letters of his name. The grooves were smooth and deep, slick with rain.

"Hi, Grandpa Henry." Tess's voice, barely a whisper, echoed in the quiet sanctuary. Henry's headstone was sturdy and upright, unlike some of the older stones in the yard. "I haven't been here for a while. I guess you know that though... I'm sorry. I'm sorry, I left and didn't say goodbye to you. I've really missed you..." Tess knelt down to the cool ground, feeling the moisture of the earth soak through her jeans to her skin. Her hands ran over the prickly blades of grass, just barely green.

"Marian – Grandma – died. I guess you know that, too." Tessa chuckled; she was not accustomed to talking with dead people and she couldn't help feeling a little silly. "She made me the executor of her will. Can you believe that? Me, who never cleaned a toilet up to her standards while I was growing up. Now she wants me to have all her money and take care of her house. Your house." Tears soaked Tess's eyes just as her knees were soaked by the earth. "I wasn't going to stay, I was going to opt out of the executor thing – but I don't know... I feel like it's my job. This is, was, my family... the only one I will ever have and I just don't want to leave it to strangers. I owe you." Tess grazed her hand over the tips of the new spikes of grass. "You probably know all this, too, don't you? I'm a little confused; I don't know what to tell you and what you already know. I don't know if you know anything, I don't know where you are, or if you even *are*... I guess I'll just talk... since I don't know the rules. I'm a lawyer now. I went to Northwestern on a scholarship. I worked through college as a seamstress at a tailor's shop... remember how Sarah Beth's mom taught me how to sew? Well, I sewed my way right through college." Tess continued on, telling Henry about her job with Chadwick, Holmes and Epstein. Then she told him about her peanut butter office and her apartment near The Loop.

"I met someone. His name is Davis... his family

owns a construction company. I think he loves – I think he *loved* me. I think I may have messed it all up though. It's so hard, ya know. I want him to love me... I want to love him back. But if I really let him in, I lose my secrets and that's... that's too big. I wish you were here. I wish I could have talked to you about my mom after I found out." Tessa stopped and took in a large breath of the wet air.

"I wish I could have talked to you after I found out Caroline killed herself. That must have been so hard for you. It must have been awful... I don't even know how awful because I don't have a daughter but I know how it felt to me." Tessa shook her body from side to side, trying to shed the memory of those feelings from her being. She had taken herself away from this town, away from Marian and had created a new life all in the name of forgetting the past and where she came from. Now here, sitting in this dark cemetery, Tessa knows that no matter how far she runs she will always be the daughter of a woman who didn't want her.

"I just wanted to say thank you. Thank you for being so good to me, even though I'm the reason that you lost your daughter. I wonder sometimes why you didn't treat me like Marian did... and then I know. You loved me. I just wanted you to know that I know now. That I've known for a long time and I'm okay. You must have put your grief on hold for so long for me... I just wanted to say that I hope the two of you are together... you and Caroline... you and my mom. And Marian. I hope Marian is with you, too. I hope she found some peace. I know I never brought her any."

Before Tessa had left Waterside she had slipped down to the beach and filled an empty bottle with water from Lake Michigan. She took the bottle out, opening the top she poured it over Henry's resting place. "I wanted to bring you something... something to bring you peace. The water, the lake, always is that place for me... because it was that place for us. You made your life and your living in that water – so I brought some of it to you." The oak trees rustled loudly as the wind picked up and now crossed Tessa's face with more force and wetness as the rain fell again in earnest. Lightning struck out over the water, illuminating the trees that lined the church, creating a lacy horizon. Tess thought of the day in Jaco Beach, the rain that had baptized her and Davis... *Henry*.

Tessa had never been sure of the afterlife. She had read somewhere that when you lose someone you love the only thing *to do* is believe in heaven – anything else hurts too much. She would like to believe that. Tessa remembered the day of Henry's funeral. Marian had not allowed her to attend; instead she dropped her off at the McGinney's where she made apple pie with Sarah Beth. She overheard Mrs. McGinney offer her condolences to Marian when they arrived. Marian had only offered a small thanks, retorting he was in a better place now. The heat Tess felt that day stuck again in her throat now as she stood to leave his grave. Tess had been angry with Marian, so angry. There was no better place for grandpa Henry than with her. Tess's young mind would not believe he would have wanted to leave her, that *he* believed any place without Tessa Wallace was a better place. It was that day that she began to doubt her spirituality, doubt that a better place could exist if she and Grandpa Henry were not together. Knowing what she knows now, Tessa smiles at the reunion of father and daughter. Yes, if there is a heaven, Henry would have welcomed it. He would have missed Tessa, she knew that, but the eternal ache of missing his daughter would have finally been soothed. Tessa closed her eyes and prayed for Marian. That the crown of grief and sorrow she wore most her life had been laid aside and Tessa prayed that Marian had finally found peace with Henry and Caroline. With her family.

Tess stood staring at his named carved in stone. She waited for a sensation, a feeling, a whisper of the wind to tell her he had heard her and felt her pain. Her disheartened soul was skeptical of the mystical and didn't believe a sign would come. Peace settled around her shoulders, a peace born of loving someone and knowing them well enough to know when they were gone that their love held stronger than time and death. She had run away from this town and her life, but she could not run away from her grandfather's love for her, or her love for him. Whether there was a heaven or not, Tess was still uncertain, but a piece of her faith in the spirituality of life was resurrected. A calm serenity draped over her. She didn't need to wonder if he heard her, if he felt her; she knew what he would say if he had. He would love her. He would protect her. She had been so busy running she couldn't see it before. She had to return home to feel it.

Knowing gave her peace. He would tell her to live her truth. To be who she was now, to celebrate who she had become.

Tessa's flashlight led her a few paces to the left where she found an identical stone to Henry's:

CAROLINE CONTESSA WALLACE
1972-1989
LOVING DAUGHTER

Tessa opened the bottle and poured the last of the water over her mother's grave, first holding the water in the palm of her hand. Water pooled between the lumps of soft, young, green moss and seeped into the earth, baptizing her mother's delicate bones. Tears mixed with rain like watercolor paint on her cheeks. Tessa cried for her mother, the hippy girl she had created to love her and the teenager who could not see past her mistakes. "Loving daughter," Tessa said. How she wished Caroline could have been defined by love instead of fear.

. . . .

Luke watched Tessa's Volvo pull away from the cemetery. He hadn't meant to follow her here. The early hours of the morning had brought a restlessness he couldn't contain, a result of fitful dreams and worry. His car led the way, winding down the familiar path on its own, knowing what would soothe his ragged soul. He had parked around the back side of the church, out of view from the road and parking lot. Tessa had arrived after he did, she didn't see his car.

The knees on his jeans were soaked through where he had knelt in prayer and peace at Caroline's grave. He had come to tell Caroline their daughter was home, Tessa was home in Chapel Corners. She was beautiful, he had said. She was beautiful and tortured, he could see that in her eyes. When he had pulled her from the icy water she had sworn it was a mistake, she hadn't thought about the temperature, she had just wanted to be in the water like she did when she was young. Fear seared through his heart like a hot poker. Suddenly his reasoning for staying away, for allowing her space to grow without the shroud of a single, young father was an ill-conceived fatalistic plan. He could not lose Tessa, not even from a distance.

Hindsight was twenty-twenty, he understood that. But today, in the light of the warmest May on record, Luke couldn't see a single reason why he would have agreed to go along with Henry and Marian's plan. He had allowed his daughter to grow up without knowing her father, without knowing the mother that only Luke knew. He had failed her, failed them both, and the pain in his daughter's eyes told him all he needed to know. There was a sadness there that he could have helped heal.

After sitting with Caroline for what felt like hours he had taken the gnarly, overgrown path down to the lake from the cemetery. He skipped rocks on the water, taking his anger out with each toss. When he had returned to his car there she was, sitting just as he had at the foot of her mother's grave. The pain was nearly more than Luke could stand. He had failed Caroline. He hadn't saved her when she believed he would. And now he was certain he had failed Tessa, his sweet daughter, too. He hadn't wanted to scare her, or worse make her feel as though she was being watched and followed. He turned back to the beach and ran. He ran as far and as fast as his legs and lungs would carry him. He ran and cried, he cursed the skies. He yelled in rage.

There was so much to be angry with. Marian! Henry! Caroline! Himself! How could he ever forgive himself for letting down his daughter, his only child? As hard as he and Cynthia had tried, they had never been able to have a child of their own. Secretly, Luke had known why. It was his penance to carry, and he had unwillingly hoisted his sadness onto Cynthia's life. He had been given a daughter, a perfect, beautiful baby girl, and he had squandered his chance to be her father. He had allowed other people — Caroline's parents and his own — to decide what would be best for her, for him. He had not followed his heart.

Honesty was all Cynthia ever asked of him, and he had given that willingly. The ache from living a life steeped in lies had made him stagnant. Cynthia had encouraged him to be honest with Tess when she was young, but Henry had threatened to take away his weekly visits. Luke lived for Tuesdays, and the thought of Henry keeping him from Tessa was too hard. He hadn't been strong enough, he hadn't been wise enough.

What about now? Was it time for him to tell Tessa the truth? Was it time for her to know he was her father?

The beholder of the truth has the power, he thought, *the power to heal, the power to forgive.* Would Tessa forgive him? Would knowing her father had loved her from her very first breath help her heal? Or would the truth weigh her down, would she feel burdened by Luke's admission? Would the truth have the power to destroy Tessa? If Luke told her now, would he be assuaging his own guilt, alleviating his own pain in exchange for his daughter's? He couldn't bear the thought of another ounce of grief poured into his daughter's heart. She had lost so much already.

By the time he made it back to his parking spot, Tessa was pulling out onto the road. He knew he didn't have much time, she wouldn't stay in Chapel Corners forever. Reenie had told him she only planned to stay at the Waterside another day or two. He had to decide what his daughter needed. Luke pulled in a deep breath and took one last look at Caroline's grave. He would do what a father should do, he would put his daughter first.

Chapter Seventeen

In some families the kitchen is the hub of activity. It is a place where good food nourishes both the body and the soul: chicken soup soothes a sore throat or warm brownies can heal hurt feelings. Mothers teach their daughters how to prepare baked beans or pizza or a baked potato. Family's legacies are passed on in kitchens.

Not for Marian Wallace.

For Marian Wallace, the kitchen was utilitarian in function and design. There were no watermelon knick-knacks, no snowmen salt and pepper shakers at Christmas or heart-shaped cookies to celebrate Saint Valentine's Day. There were white dishtowels that were easy to bleach, sturdy silverware, one oak clock, a small table to serve meals, and an old, mustard yellow rotary phone with a pen and notepad to record messages. The fridge never displayed a magnet, photograph or a child's coveted artwork. It was a place to work, to provide meals and organize life.

That is where Tess began dismantling her childhood home. There wasn't much personal about a pastry blender or half-a-box of cornstarch. Tess had not once been given a cooking lesson or learned how to make her great-grandmother's lemon bars, so there were no memories to haunt her and nothing to get in the way of progress. Tess worked quickly. The kitchen took four and a half hours to whittle through. She had nine piles for the Volunteers of America, four boxes of dry and canned goods for the food bank, and five boxes of kitchen utensils, pots and pans, small appliances, dishes and silverware.

Starving and unwilling to eat in Marian's house, Tessa dusted off her Meijer jeans and slid her gym shoes on her feet. The new McDonald's in Chapel Corners was only a few blocks away. Tessa could eat and be back at Front Street pulling apart the remains of Marian Wallace's life in thirty minutes. She pulled her Chicago Cubs baseball hat down over her head and walked across the Oriental rug in front of the front door. Just as she pulled the door shut behind her, a white minivan pulled into the cracked and mottled concrete driveway, parking just behind Tessa's Volvo. A blonde woman with her hair pulled into a ponytail on top of her head hopped out of the van.

"Sarah Beth McGinney!" Tessa hollered.

"Sarah Beth *Wagner* now, girl! How are you?" The two women quickly stepped into a hug. Sarah Beth was rounder, softer and still beautiful. Time and marriage had treated her well. The women held each other in an affectionate and familiar, if hesitant, embrace. Sarah Beth's blue eyes sparkled with tears as the two friends pulled away and laughed as the time and distance that had separated them melted like ice cream. "You don't look any different!"

"Neither do you! How are you? You're married?" Tessa noticed two car seats in the minivan behind them. She suddenly wanted to know everything, to hear every detail of her oldest friend's life.

"I'm married, six years ago now. Jimmy and I have two girls, Zoe is four and Madeline is one. What about you? How are you? Are you married?" The questions and answers seemed to fly around the two women hanging in the air like dandelion seeds suspended in a slow breeze.

"How'd you know I was here?"

"Please, Tessa Wallace. Don't tell me you've forgotten that much about livin' in The Corners; privacy is a foreign concept in this little town!" Tessa and Sarah Beth laughed.

"Are you hungry? Do you want to get some lunch?" Tessa's stomach was now growling loudly.

"I'd love to, actually. I asked my mom to keep the girls for a couple hours so I could try and catch up with you before you left again. I heard you were cleaning out the house, I thought maybe you'd like some help."

"Oh your mom! I miss your mom. I am so happy to see you, but are you sure you want to spend your baby-free time cleaning out ol' Marian's tomb?"

"Probably about as much as you want to spend your time doing it! And I do want to spend time with you. That's what friends are for, right?" Sarah Beth's smile was genuine. They had been as close as sisters for fifteen years before Tessa left. "Where do you want to eat?"

"I don't know. You pick! You know this place best these days."

"I have an idea." Sarah Beth spun around and jogged to her side of the van, opening the creaky door again. "Get in. Let's go." Sarah Beth's van was littered with mommy paraphernalia. A pacifier on a string was clipped to the rear-view mirror, the carpet was decorated with multi-colored juice stains and a pile of board books, a box of diaper wipes, and a sippy cup clogged the space between the two front seats.

"Sorry about the mess, we seem to live in this van!" Sarah Beth cast her eyes downward.

"No, no, it's fine. It's wonderful actually. Signs of life." Tessa smiled at Sarah Beth and they drove down Front Street, across to Main and headed out of town. Sarah Beth and Tessa talked freely of motherhood, marriage and law school. All the basic details they had missed out on with each other. They drove on until finally Tess realized where they were headed.

The road was as familiar to Tess as her office at CH&E, its curves romantic and beautiful. Oak trees centuries old lined the road, creating a tunnel with their giant boughs hanging well into the middle of the road. The leaves, small sprouts of green, were promising and hopeful; spring was here and summer would come. The hill that led to the orchard was steep. The ditches were filled with volunteer daffodils and lavender patches of lilac bushes quilted the fence rows. Tessa suddenly felt overwhelmed with fatigue. Sarah Beth chatted furiously (Tessa was happy to see that had not changed) about the ins and outs of her life with the girls: preschool on Tuesdays and Thursdays for Zoe, and on Mondays she took them both to swimming lessons at the new aquatic center in Covington. Being a stay-at-home mom was hard, she wanted to pull her hair out at least once most days, but her mom was there and that saved her. She hardly missed her job at Dr. Bailey's office at all. Tessa thought of Reenie and hoped that Sarah Beth was authentically happy about her choice to stay with her children. It saddened her that she may be longing for something underneath this bubbly exterior.

"How are your mom and dad?"

"Mom's fine, she still keeps her hand in running the farmer's market. They added a deli about five years ago, homemade sandwiches and potato salads, fresh pies and fruit of course… that's where I thought we'd eat lunch."

"Oh wow! That sounds great. What about your dad?"

"We lost my dad three years ago."

"Oh Sarah Beth, I'm so sorry." Seth McGinney was a good man, he and his daughter had been close. Tess's stomach lurched around her hunger, she had allowed Marian to take so much from her. Sarah Beth had been married, had two daughters and lost her father — and Tess had been there for none of it.

"He had a massive heart attack in the back grove just about this time of year. Jimmy was with him, but he just couldn't get him up to the house in time." Sarah Beth dabbed at her wet eyes with the corner of her sweatshirt. "The doctor in the ER said it wouldn't have mattered, he was gone within seconds."

"I can't believe all that's happened to you since I left. All I did was go to law school and get a job!" Tess's regret was louder than her words. Sarah Beth and her family had been the one rock solid thing in her life after Grandpa Henry died, and she had repaid them by dropping completely out of their lives. Tessa reached across and held Sarah Beth's hand in her own. Sarah Beth squeezed her hand back. Tessa thought of the lake and how friendship was like the waves. The good ones, the strong ones, are always there, ebbing and flowing with the pull of the tide. When you reach out, they are always waiting, ever faithful.

The old farm house that Sarah Beth had grown up in had been converted into a deli and gift shop. Inside there were a few customers, a group of gray-haired, pot-bellied men gathered around four steaming cups of brewed coffee each eating a slice of pie. Another table held two women around Tess's age, both with young babies, one a boy the other a girl. The two women were chatting easily while pacifying their children with sips from bottles, bites of food from their plates, wagging rattles and storybooks in their view all while they gently touched and soothed and talked. The store was on the right and smelled exactly like Mrs. McGinney's kitchen did when the girls grew up — homespun. The lights were dim and there were dried flowers hanging from the ceiling. Flower arrangements lined along the walls with dried fruit, flowers and grapevine bases.

"Wow! This place has changed so much!"

"Yeah, Jimmy was working here with Dad and now he's been running it. He had a bigger vision... still does actually. He bought the equipment a few years back to press cider, so we do that in the fall and now at Christmas we also sell trees, wreaths and give holiday sleigh rides through the orchard. He has started growing grapes in the back acres of the property and has plans to make wine. Did you see the flowers outside?"

"No, I didn't," Tess replied.

"He brought in annuals and some perennials, too. He loves it here."

"I'm so glad, it sounds as if you are all really happy."

"Losing Dad was just so hard... well you remember when you lost your Grandpa what it feels like? You just don't know if that blue feeling will ever go away. Luckily, though, I had Zoe already and had Maddy soon after. They saved me... Mom, too." Sarah Beth smiled at Tessa. "Let's eat. I know you are starving."

The two women feasted on egg salad sandwiches on homemade whole wheat bread with fresh potato salad, raspberry tea and each had a slice of peach pie. The food filled Tess in a way she had not been satiated in days. McGinney's Deli, in the middle of the orchard that Tessa knew so well, felt more like home to her than Front Street or Chicago.

"Momma!" Sarah Beth swept around in her seat at the sound of her daughter's voice.

"Zoe! What are you doin' here baby girl?" Sarah Beth gobbled up the little girl with her long arms. "Where's Grandma? Where's Maddy?"

"Gramma's in da back wit Maddy. She said we had to wun an erwand."

"You had to run an errand with Grandma?" Sarah Beth smiled. "Zoe, this is Momma's friend Miss Tessa. Can you say 'hi' to Miss Tessa?" Zoe whispered a thin 'hi' as she tucked her head in under her mother's arm.

"Hi, Zoe. It is so nice to meet you. You sure have a pretty dress on." Zoe spun her yellow sundress with bright pink flowers embroidered on the hemline from side to side while she smiled sideways at Tessa.

"Tank you."

"What good manners, Zoe girl. Let's go find Grandma, okay?" Sarah Beth stood easily with her daughter nestled in her side while she looked around the small deli and into the back kitchen area. "Mom?"

"Sarah Beth?"

"Hey, Mom. Somebody's here to see you!" Sarah Beth said. Elizabeth McGinney walked around the corner.

"Tessa Wallace, my goodness it is so good to see you, sweetheart!" Elizabeth held Tessa in a tight hug. The stocky, solid woman was shorter than when Tessa left. Her hair was still red and her wrinkles were few; she had spent her life working the trees and land and this business that she loves. Shadows pooled in her hazel eyes; the sadness from losing the love of her life lived there. Mr. and Mrs. McGinney had adored each other. She held her younger granddaughter, Maddy, on her ample hip and the infant reached for her mother.

"Hello, Mrs. McGinney. Lunch was wonderful. The deli, the orchard, everything looks just wonderful."

"I'm so glad you girls connected, and that you got to come back out to the orchard. I'm so sorry to hear about your grandmother."

Tessa smiled simply. "Thank you. Sarah Beth has just been filling me in on everything here... I can't tell you how sad I am about Mr. McGinney."

"It's a part of me every day. But my girls help, all three of them." Elizabeth squeezed Maddy as she leaned slightly into Sarah Beth, a sad smile settled on her face. The three women chatted at the deli counter, Tessa gave Elizabeth the highlights of her education and career while Zoe wandered toward the store looking at the few handmade puzzles on the shelf under the cash register. Maddy melted into her mother's arms and her eyes closed as the women chatted.

Tessa fit into the McGinney house like a key in a lock. She would spend day after day, night after night. And when it was finally time to go home, she would beg Mrs. McGinney not to take her. Tessa traveled on a few family vacations with the trio, the Smokey Mountains once and Sarasota, Florida twice to visit Seth McGinney's mother. A decade later, Tessa stood inside the home they had turned into a charming cafe and watched the two women holding Sarah Beth's young daughters. Tessa was sad. Sarah Beth had grown a family, and her mother was there with her, watching and helping and loving both generations of her own.

In a sudden maternal wave, Tessa wanted to hold little Maddy, touch her sweet skin and brush her red bangs out of her eyes. She wanted to tell Zoe stories of her momma and walk with her in the orchard like she and Sarah Beth had done as little girls. Tessa watched the circle of life that she had not been given and had not created for herself, a circle of mothers and daughters. It physically pained Tessa as she listened to Sarah Beth and Elizabeth organize the rest of the girls' afternoon and evening care. Her brilliant green eyes pooled with wistful tears.

Mrs. McGinney offered to take the girls back to her house for naps so Jimmy could come collect them after dinner and Sarah would head back to Marian's to help Tessa clean out the old house. Before they left Tessa asked if they could take a quick walk around the orchard, and Sarah smiled. "Absolutely."

The sun warmed the women's shoulders as they walked. The breeze was gentle with just a twist of the chill of winter left. The apple trees were pregnant with blossoms beginning to appear, and soon the smell of apple would be heavy in the air. "Where are you living now?" Tessa asked.

"We built a house up the road, right next to my mom. She and Dad built a new house up there a few years before he died. Jimmy and I lived in town for a few years but then after my dad died. We decided it would be better to be closer to the orchard, closer to Mom. It's good, most days Jimmy comes home for lunch, which he wouldn't be able to do if we were still in town. I like that, gives me a break and I get to see my man." She smiled.

"Are you happy?" Tessa asked. In all of their late-night adolescent girl sleepover talks, Sarah Beth had wanted to get out, get away from Chapel Corners and see what the world had to offer.

"I like how the trees all look the same. Ya know, they just don't change much. And when they do, they change in the same ways every year. They are predictable. Funny, no one has asked me if I'm happy in years... maybe ever." Sarah Beth paused, contemplating her answer. "Yes, I'm happy. I love Jimmy. He's wonderful to me and a great dad. He drives me nuts sometimes, when he won't pick up his socks or sleeps on the couch while I fold laundry or loses his temper, but most days he makes me happy. And the girls... the girls are what I was put on this Earth to do. Sometimes I wish I had more time for myself, but when I go out with a friend for dinner, or go shop with my mom, I am anxious to come home. Once I finally head back to Jimmy and the girls, I can't wait to see my house in the distance up on the hill and make my last turn toward home. That's where I want to be. It didn't take me long to realize that this is it for me: the orchard, Jimmy, the girls, being close to my momma. So, yes. All that dreaming we did about leaving this old town just wasn't meant for me after all. But you! Are you happy?"

Tessa ducked under a branch from the apple tree in front of her, brushing it gently with her shoulder. "Oh... Sarah Beth. Am I happy?" Tess pondered in silence as Sarah Beth walked next to her, matching her step for step. "I thought I was. Content at least. I thought if I left this all behind, left *Marian* behind, I would get past it and could *become* happy. But, Marian showed up at my office last Monday when Roger Lanford called me to tell me she was dead and now everything feels different." Tessa kept walking, touching branches as she passed by them. "At the time I left I didn't see any other way except to leave Chapel Corners, I didn't think I had a choice. I had to get away from Marian and the only way to do that was to run.

It took me coming back to realize I also let go of a lot of good memories and people."

Tess and Sarah Beth had reached the top of the highest point of the orchard. Both women paused to take in the view, breathing hard. Sarah Beth sat down on the bench that had crowned this hill since they were girls. The view was expansive. The orchard sprawled out underneath them on sloping hills, and soon the pink blossoms would trim the picture with confetti. Lake Michigan shimmered on the horizon and Sarah Beth sat next to Tessa quietly.

"I used to dream about her up here. I dreamt about my mom so many times on top of this hill." Tessa's voice faded.

"Why'd you leave, Tessa?" Sarah Beth's voice was gentle.

"It's so complicated," Tessa answered.

"I'm not sure I know much about adulting that isn't complicated." Sarah Beth smiled.

Tessa's eyes looked down softly. "My mom killed herself." Sarah Beth was stunned into silence. "I always thought she died in childbirth, that's what Grandpa Henry told me when I was old enough to ask questions. But she didn't. She died three weeks after I was born, she purposefully overdosed on pain pills."

"What in the hell are you talking about, Tessa?" Sarah Beth stared at her oldest friend in disbelief. "How do you know that? Who told you that?"

"Marian. My grandma told me that. She kept it from me all those years and let me think Caroline died giving birth to me. I always assumed that's why Marian treated me the way she did, I always figured Marian believed I was the reason her daughter died. In a twisted way I understood. The reality is that Marian protected me from the truth all those years. The truth is my mom, Caroline, took her own life three weeks after she gave me mine."

"I don't know, Tessa. I don't know. I never heard that before. This is a small town, I would have heard that before!" The news had hit Sarah Beth as all difficult things do, with denial.

"I found her death certificate," Tessa cried. "It's true."

"Oh Tessa… Oh Tessa, I'm so sorry." Sarah Beth cried with her friend and held her hand.

"Marian said it was my fault. She told me she killed herself because she was so embarrassed to have gotten pregnant. She was ashamed. If it weren't for me, she would still be alive." Tess was sobbing now. She had never spoken the words out loud, never told another soul what Marian had said to her that night. The comfort from sharing her burden was overwhelming. The relief came in waves, the weight on her shoulders lessened. Ten years of carrying the truth alone was over.

"Tessa, tell me you don't believe that. That's ridiculous. It's not true." Sarah Beth held both of Tessa's hands in her own. "It's not true!" She shook Tess until Tessa looked her in the eyes.

"It is true! Marian said it, she believed it, she was her mother, she knew!"

"I am a mother. I am telling you with everything I

have and everything I know, Caroline may have taken her own life, but she did not take it because of you." Sarah Beth was indignant. "Goddamnit! How could she say that to you? That's why you left, isn't it? It's why you walked out of all of our lives, because Marian told you that!"

"It was so awful. It *is* so awful. Do you know what it's like to *know* your mom didn't love you enough to stay? Didn't love you enough to want to be with you, to love you every day?" Tessa's shoulders heaved with sobs and grief. A decade's worth of shame and worry spilled out on top of the apple orchard hill. "Marian was so angry. She slapped me across the face and I left. I spent the night driving around town, and that's when I decided I would leave. I would leave Chapel Corners and create a new life. Be a new Tessa Wallace. I would just start over." Sarah Beth wrapped her arm around Tessa and Tessa rested her head on Sarah Beth's shoulder. The late afternoon sun warmed their heads. "I'm sorry. I'm so sorry I never called you, or wrote you... or tried at all. I just couldn't..." Tess's sobs began to settle.

"My dear, sweet friend. Listen to me. I don't know why Caroline decided to take those pills, I have no idea. But I do know, are you listening?" Sarah Beth urged Tessa to look her in the eye. "I know that a mother doesn't leave her daughter. Not on purpose, not without thinking it was what was best for you. I know that in my heart."

"The thing is... she knew. My mom knew what it was going to be like for me to grow up with Marian and she left me with her anyway."

"She left you with Grandpa Henry, too," Sarah Beth reminded Tessa.

Tessa smiled. "Yes, she did. I never longed for a father like I longed for my mother. He filled those shoes."

"Grandpa Henry was awesome. He really was. And maybe, maybe Marian wasn't like... well, like she was... before Caroline died." Sarah Beth took a deep breath. "It's a mother's greatest fear, from the day your baby is born until the day you die, your greatest fear as a mom is that your child will die before you. I never had much sympathy for Marian as a young girl, and I don't have a lot now, except... except for the fact that it's hard for me to judge a woman who lost her child. I don't know who I would become, how I would behave, what I would be capable of, if I lost one of my girls. I never looked at it this way until now, and to know she willingly took her life would almost be too much to bear."

"I have thought of that a lot since I came back into town. I acted like I owned Caroline. I owned her memory and the grief and sadness that went with losing her." Tessa tucked her hands underneath her legs on the bench. "I didn't give Marian much reason to love me, honestly."

"Well, that's not true. Being you is enough reason to love you but I think I understand what you are saying. I wish you would have come here that night. Why didn't you?"

"You know, it never crossed my mind. After Grandpa Henry died, you and your mom and dad had been my safe place to fall, my favorite place to be. I was so shocked, so hurt, I didn't feel I could be around anyone. I was so wounded I nearly broke. It nearly broke me."

"I supposed this is where I say, I understand. But I don't, so I won't. I will just tell you that I wish I had known. I wish I could have told you a decade ago that your mom did not take those pills to get away from you." Sarah Beth was certain.

"We don't know that. The truth is all I have, all I have is Marian's word. I have nothing else. I know you would never do that, of course you wouldn't, but the only real thing I know about my mother is that she was pregnant at seventeen and she took her own life three weeks after I was born. That's all I know for sure." Sarah Beth nodded as Tess spoke, understanding that for today it would have to be enough that she shared her sadness. "Do you remember how I asked your dad once about why the apple trees were shaped so funny? Why they weren't pretty and round like the apple trees in books?"

"I don't remember that…"

"I asked him why they were so crazy looking, why they grew in such crazy directions. He told me that when a limb grew into the space of another limb and began to rub, it made the tree vulnerable. The tree could get an infection in the wounded area where the two limbs rubbed and it would compromise the whole tree."

"I do remember now!"

"He pruned the trees. He cut away the limbs that rubbed together so that they wouldn't do damage to the whole tree. I asked him if it was bad for the tree why it decided to grow its limbs that way and he laughed at me.

He said he didn't think that the tree was probably that smart." Tessa smiled.

"He loved you, too," Sarah Beth said.

"I know he did," Tessa answered. The two friends sat quietly for a few moments. "Do you know what I want? What would make me happy?"

Sarah Beth lifted her eyes in answer to Tess's question. "What would make you happy?"

"I want a last turn home."

Chapter Eighteen

Back at Front Street, Tessa and Sarah Beth worked their way through the two bathrooms and the spare bedroom. Tessa had found a bottle of Old Spice, Grandpa Henry's favorite, which she put in her "keep" pile. Sarah Beth had gone through the kitchen boxes, saving a Crock Pot and two tablecloths.

Tessa talked. She talked as if her life depended on it. She talked about Adrianna and the O'Learys. She told Sarah Beth about Holmes and her Five-Year plan. She talked about Davis and Jaco Beach. Her decade-long silence was over, and she was an open flood gate. The heaviness from earlier in the day lifted as the two friends packed and laughed together, listening to Bon Jovi and Earl Thomas Connely on Spotify. Tessa felt energized, she was lighter.

As dusk fell upon Chapel Corners, Sarah Beth and Tess collapsed on the couch in the still-intact living room. The midnight blue carpet buffered the remaining light, leaving the two in the dark. Between the two of them sat a small box marked "THW." Sarah Beth had found it in the far back corner of the hall closet earlier in the day. The tape crackled as Tess sliced through it with an X-acto knife, leaving the cardboard to shear open. Inside Tess found an emery board, two AA batteries, an eraser shaped like a strawberry that held vague traces of its fruity scent, and a ticket stub from the Sun movie theatre in downtown Chapel Corners.

"What is this stuff? Did she empty out a junk drawer and mark your initials on it?" Sarah Beth quipped.

"No, I remember the eraser. This was stuff from my bedside table. Who in the world would go through the trouble of saving this junk?" Tess continued to pull out miscellaneous items from the box, including a bottle of hand lotion, a pack of gum and a few hair ties.

"Oh, remember these?" Sarah Beth threw the orange-and-blue patterned scrunchie around her ponytail.

"We wore these all the time!" Tessa's eyes lit up.

"Look at this! I can't believe she saved these!" Tess pulled out a small gray bag and unzipped it. Inside was Tess's box of tarot cards. "Do you remember when I bought these in that funky, little bookstore in downtown Covington?"

"Oh my gosh, yes, I do! It was right after Grandpa Henry died and we thought he could send us a message through them – here, do me!"

"I don't know if I remember what any of them mean! Is the book in here, too?" Tessa sifted through the box, eventually finding *The Guide to Tarot Cards* underneath a *Seventeen* magazine. "Here, draw one!" Sarah Beth held her hands out and pinched a card from the deck.

"Hmmm… the three of pentacles, what's that mean?"

"I know the three represents an initial completion, or success." Tessa flipped through the guidebook until she found the description of the three of pentacles. "Here we go. The cyclical cards represent the ending of one phase, the beginning of another." Tess smiled as she turned the boldly drawn picture over in her hands. Purples, oranges, reds, and blues all graced the scenes on the card. She found their glimpses of another time comforting now, much like she had as a girl.

"Like us," Sarah Beth said. "We found each other again, the last ten years we've been apart. Now we have the chance to be close again." Sarah Beth was tentative with her words.

"Just like us." Tessa smiled at Sarah Beth. She had bought the cards on a lark. As a young girl she had so desperately wanted to be connected with Henry and Caroline that she tried many avenues of spirituality. She had felt such anger at Henry's death that her faith in God had been shattered. No God who loved her the way she had been taught would have taken Henry away and left her to survive with Marian. So began her quest to find another answer. The cards had been one step in a long line of psychics, prophets, church groups and a brief stay with Buddhism. Eventually, Tess had given up, left all of her sentiments behind, and relied on herself and her intelligence to pull herself through.

"Your turn." Sarah Beth tucked her legs under her bottom.

"King of Pentacles," Tessa announced. Thinking for a moment, she began to giggle. "I think his keywords are achievement, workaholic, financially successful. Everything I am. All I am." Tess's words started boldly and faded.

"That's not all you are. You're funny, and sad. You like music and pizza. You love your job, and you love Davis." The true weight of her sadness cradled Tess in the darkness of her childhood home. She had been running so long and so fast she had almost forgotten why. Now she remembered. The heartbreak of losing her mother, twice, and Henry and Sarah Beth was so much harder to feel if she just kept moving forward. Sarah Beth reached and held her hand. "Draw another one."

"I can't. This is all there is for me. I know it. It's all I've created. I'm successful, I'm financially comfortable. I'm independent and I'm good at what I do. I haven't done anything to build what you and Jimmy have. If anything, I have done everything to avoid it. The cards are right, this is me." Sarah Beth reached into the stack of cards and pulled one for Tessa.

"Queen of Swords," Sarah Beth said.

"She's seen as someone who has experienced sorrow and bears her pain with courage. Always ready to cut away untruths. An articulate truth-speaker, she's experienced enough not to rush too fast into an emotional relationship." Tessa looked at the ceiling, the tension and fear of the day draining from her face. "How do they *do* that?" Tessa questioned the cards.

Sarah Beth laughed. "I have no idea but it's crazy how spot on that just was."

Tessa continued to dig through the box, collecting trash to throw away and deciding what to keep. Near the bottom of the box was an envelope with a letter tucked inside that Tessa didn't recognize. The paper slid out from the envelope with ease, as if it wanted to be read. Scanning the words, Tessa felt a lump in her throat. She pushed the paper back into the envelope as quickly as she had pulled them out. She wasn't ready to read it yet, she needed time to think and to be alone.

"What's that?" Sarah Beth asked.

"Who knows? She saved a lot of stuff." Tessa laughed and closed the box up. "I'll take this one back with me to the hotel and go through it later."

"Hello?" An unfamiliar male voice echoed down the hall of Marian's home.

"Jimmy?" Sarah Beth sat up from her lounged position with her legs flung loosely over the arm of the loveseat. Tessa craned her neck backward.

"Sarah Beth?"

"We're back here, honey. What are you doing here?" Even in the darkness Tessa could see the glow that loving her husband gave to Sarah Beth. Jimmy rounded the corner into the dark at the back of the house. Tessa sat up to greet him just in time to watch him kiss his wife hello.

"I thought you two girls could use a break. I brought the leftover fried chicken your mom made for dinner, some coleslaw and a few biscuits. Your mom came down to put the girls to bed at home so I could come catch up with you... I hope that's okay. I'm not intruding on your girl time, am I?" Jimmy smiled at his wife, kissing her on her nose.

"No, not at all," Tessa answered for Sarah Beth. "Hi, Jimmy, it's so nice to meet you. I'm Tessa and I'm starving, so I'm thrilled about Mrs. McGinney's chicken!"

"Likewise, I've heard a lot about you over the years. Welcome home." The sentiment hung in the air like a day-old helium balloon. Was she home? "I also brought a bottle of wine, anybody care for some with dinner?" Jimmy's tall frame bent to unload the contents of the picnic basket he had carried in.

"Let's head outside, we can eat out on the back deck, enjoy the last of the evening," Tessa suggested.

The backyard had always been one of her favorite places in this house. Henry had kept a garden in the southeast corner of the lot. She loved the fresh cherry tomatoes early in the morning, the insides warm from the sun, seeds and pulp gushing into your mouth when you bit down. A mulberry tree grew in the back, hiding the fence that they shared with the neighbors to the south. She would climb that tree and sit for hours, staining her hands with the sweet purple juice. She had some happy times here, and they were easier to see when she stopped running. Before Jimmy had brought over dinner Tessa had looked for the ferns that Henry had transplanted under the mulberry tree from his father's backyard after he passed away. A few tender fronds made their way up through the accumulated debris of the fall and winter, looking like a strand of yellow-green pearls reaching upward. Tessa had cleared away some of the sticks, discarded nut cases, old leaves and mulch to give them an easier push.

Tessa, Sarah Beth and Jimmy dined on Elizabeth McGinney's home-cooked meal heartily. Jimmy inquired about Tess's job at CH&E, Chicago, and what it was like to live in a big city after growing up in The Corners. Jimmy had grown up in Novi, a suburb of Detroit, met Sarah Beth at Hope College and moved into small town life here in Chapel Corners. He was kind and authentic and Tessa found him similar to Davis in a small-town way. Tessa noted Jimmy's strong jaw and long sturdy nose; his eyes were almond brown and wide set. His brown hair was long enough to curl above his eyes in a charming boyish fashion. Watching Sarah Beth and Jimmy together, Tessa continued to question her choices. She had given up a marriage and family with Mark Norman for her job at CH&E and now her relationship with Davis had stalled because she ran away. Was that what she wanted?

"That was so good, I am so full." Tess stretched backward in her chair reaching her arms up above her head. The day's work and the wine combined to make her relaxed and sleepy.

"I am too," Sarah Beth and Jimmy said in unison. Tessa laughed. Dusk had finished settling as dinner began, the lavender hour had come and gone.

"Is the playhouse still out there, Tessa?"

"It is. I haven't been out there, though. I don't know what kind of shape it's in." Tessa swatted a mosquito away from her ankle.

"Do you remember how much fun we had in that little house? We used to play 'house' and 'school' with our baby dolls. We hid from Grandma Marian out there, too… remember?" Jimmy quietly sipped his wine as he had most of the evening, soaking in the tales of a decade-old friendship that had helped to shape his wife.

"She would never come out to get us. Do you remember that? It's like she was afraid of the grass or sun or something," Tessa added, brow furrowed, remembering.

"She probably was afraid. She was probably a vampire." Sarah Beth was the one soul on this Earth who knew what it was really like to be Marian Wallace's granddaughter and it felt good and safe to be in her company. "We had fun out there, though. I wish my girls had a place like that."

"Take it," Tessa said. "Jimmy, can you move something like that? I think it's just like a little wooden box with a roof." Tessa sat up in her chair. Giving Sarah Beth the playhouse would create a connection for her, and start new memories in that old building that held her sorrow.

"I don't know if you could move it, I'd have to look and see," Jimmy replied thoughtfully.

"Let's look now." Tessa stood up turning on the flashlight in her phone.

Jimmy lumbered up slowly as Tess had discovered was his way. He was slow and purposeful in his movements, almost graceful. The two women were quickly walking the twenty paces to the back of the lot with Jimmy a few steps behind. The outside was painted pink with blue gingerbread trim and had two real windows on the sides and a front door that opened onto a small covered porch; the paint had faded, even chipped a little, but the walls and roof were straight. Tessa and

Sarah Beth were both still small enough to go inside, while Jimmy (at six-foot two) looked around the outside and into the windows, surveying the plausibility of moving the house.

"Sarah Beth, look, it's just like it used to be… it hasn't been touched in years!" The small table that occupied the corner with two tiny pink chairs was covered in mouse droppings. On the opposite wall the little girl-sized china hutch that Grandpa Henry had made Tessa for Christmas one year still stood with a few small tea cups hanging from aged brass hooks.

"Look at the wall, Tessa!" There, written in third grade script, was *Tessa Wallace and Sarah Beth McGinney B/F/F!* "Can you believe it's still here? After all this time…" Tessa looked over her friend's shoulder, resting her chin there while she looked at the promise the two little girls had made to each other.

"I can't believe I am standing in this playhouse with you again after all these years." Tessa became weepy as she turned her attention back to the small china cabinet. She gently tugged at the swollen doors, bracing the top of the hutch with her opposite hand. The cupboard finally broke free and Tess shone her light onto the shelves. The coasters that belonged to the three tea cups were tucked inside, laced together with spider webbing. "You girls making tea in there or what?" Jimmy smiled from outside the playhouse.

"Yeah, Jimmy… we're coming right out." Tess crouched to exit the playhouse, Sarah Beth was right behind her. "What do you think? Do you think you can move it?"

"I think maybe... it looks like it was built in sections... maybe it could be taken apart and transported that way and put back together—"

"I'll pay to have it done, and have a fresh coat of paint put on the outside. And the furniture inside, too. Whatever color Zoe wants."

"Tessa..." Sarah Beth began.

"No, I want to. My grandpa made this playhouse for my mother, and then you and I loved it. Your girls should have it... and they can't play with it here and they can't play with it with mouse poop on the tables. Really... let me. It's the least I can do... the two of you disrupted your lives for me as soon as I blew back into town. I want to." Tessa's eyes brimmed with tears. At that moment, more than anything in the world, she needed to see the restoration of the little blue house for her best friend's daughters. Mending souls can sometimes start with mending fences. "I know Jimmy you could probably do it yourself, but you're so busy at the orchard. I'll call around and find a guy. I'll find a guy to do it. It would mean so much to me to know those two little girls are having tea parties and playing house and you know... doing sister stuff."

"That's very sweet... the girls would love it." Jimmy reached across the dark and pulled Tessa toward him in half a hug. "If Aunt Tessa wants to give them a playhouse, then a playhouse they will have." Tessa's eyes welled with tears again.

"Tessa... are you okay?" Sarah Beth's brow pulled

together in concern.

"I'm okay… really, I am. It's just been a lot of stuff this week. A lot of tough stuff… and some really wonderful stuff." Tessa's mouth curled in a smile. Adrianna had played the role of her best friend in Chicago, but being back here on Front Street with Sarah Beth had reminded Tessa what friendship could be. Tessa had given up so much when she cut ties with Marian. One of the biggest casualties was her love for Sarah Beth, who had befriended her during her lonely, sad years as a girl and then young woman. Tess had not felt this kind of warmth or support from another woman for years. It was a safe place to be. The two women embraced tightly, soaking in their lost years.

Tess, Sarah Beth and Jimmy cleaned up dinner off the back patio, shut Marian's house down and said their goodbyes at the front walk. Jimmy wrapped Tessa in a hug meant to soothe her. He was a good man. Sarah Beth cried and made Tessa promise not to leave town without a goodbye. Tessa reiterated her promise to organize the moving of the playhouse and told Jimmy and Sarah Beth that she would track them down over hell and high water before she left town again. Appeased by this, Sarah Beth climbed into her minivan, door creaking shut behind her while Jimmy pulled out in front of her in his green pickup truck. Both vehicles honked as they drove away.

Tessa grabbed the small box marked "THW" and her purse from inside her Volvo, locked the vehicle and began walking toward the Waterside Inn. The night was chilly, persuading her to pull on her Meijer sweatshirt over her dirty T-shirt. A walk was exactly what she needed, a respite and time to think.

Step after step passed as Tessa quietly made her way into the dark and away from Marian's front porch light. Somehow, in the past three days her life left its predictable path and catapulted her into the past so deeply she was having a hard time remembering her life in Chicago. Tess tried to envision her peanut butter office at CH&E, the sound the water fountain draped over the entryway of the law offices, her apartment, Davis's brownstone, the Lake from the other side… none of it came to her, none of it except Davis's face.

Watching Sarah Beth with Jimmy tonight, and earlier observing Elizabeth with Sarah Beth, Zoe and Maddy, Tessa felt a strong void. Her body ached for the warmth she found with Davis, the tie they shared after the CAO benefit last week. Tessa pulled out her cell phone, brushing her hand against the letter, turned it on, and dialed his number. Voicemail. She hung up without leaving a message. He probably quit taking her phone calls. She couldn't blame him. She'd been foolish and now regretted it. She turned her phone back off, not wanting to feel the pain of him not returning her call.

Why was she still here? What made her stay? Tessa felt herself falling into her old life, being haunted by her old questions. The letter buried in the box of junk confused her even further. Was she supposed to read it? Let it be? She had scanned the letter quickly enough to realize it was written by her mother, Caroline, and that it was written to her, Tessa. Tess was unsure if she wanted to know what the letter said, but also, she had never held something in her own hands that had been so deeply connected to her mother. The chance to run her hands along the handwritten pages where Caroline's skin had rested was tempting, the physicality of it enormous.

Tessa still didn't know what to do with the letter when she reached the Waterside.

Reenie was at the front desk when Tessa walked into the now-familiar lobby. Today her purple scarf was draped around her neck from the front and lay quietly draped down her back. She was intently working on a crossword puzzle. "Hi, Reenie," Tessa said.

"Hi, dear. How are you? Did you get some work done at your grandmother's?" Reenie continued to fill in words of the puzzle at a rapid pace.

"Yeah, yeah I did." Tess plopped her elbows down on the front counter, resting her chin on her forearms as they collapsed. She peered down at the squares and letters in Reenie's hand. "There's so much to do, and I have to go home sometime… soon." Tess's stomach tightened. "I'll try and get through my grandpa's den tomorrow and then hire movers or something. I just really want to make sure I have taken care of his things."

"He was important to you," Reenie said.

"Yep, he was. Very. Hey, Reenie… can I ask you a question?"

"Of course, Tessa." Reenie stopped writing and put the puzzle book down, looking up squarely into Tess's eyes. At first this directness had bothered Tess, but she had come to find the quirk endearing, comforting.

"If you knew something about your past that really hurt you, and you happened upon more information about that past... would you look into it?" The question was cryptic, Tess knew, but she could not bear to reveal that Caroline had committed suicide to avoid being her mother, and she couldn't decide to read the letter on her own.

"Hmmm... that's not much to go on, dear." Reenie adjusted her scarf and moved the pencil out of the crease of the puzzle book and closed it. "I think you — I think *I* would have to decide if that information would bring me peace, if it would lay to rest what had hurt me."

"Yeah... probably," was all the answer Tess could gather together.

Chapter Nineteen

In her room, Tess kicked off her gym shoes, changed into her last clean T-shirt from Meijer, brushed her teeth and put her hair up in a high ponytail. Pulling back the green and purple gladiolas on the bedspread in room 111, Tess snuggled the pillows from both double beds up around her back and sat crisscross, laying the box in her lap. She pulled the envelope out of its nest and turned it around in her hands, touching each side of the letter. She had looked at it so quickly with Sarah Beth at the house, she hadn't been prepared to read it in front of anyone. Now that she was alone, she was afraid it wasn't what she thought it might be. If it's true, if it's what she thinks it is, Tessa's life will change. Nothing will be the same.

The paper slipped out of the envelope with ease.

September 27, 1989

I know my sweet little Tessa that you will probably never read this. But I don't know what else to do. I can't go on with my life pretending like you were never here and I never touched you and that you never touched me. Being your mother, even for just those five days, was the best thing that ever happened to me. You showed me perfect love. I hope you grow to be a strong, happy girl and that you have a family that loves you. I know that if you have tried to find me that you are probably sad that I am gone, but I am just not this strong. I can't stay and live out my life without you and your father, you both filled me with such love that the emptiness is swallowing me. I sang you this song every night before you fell asleep for the four nights I held you, and I have sung it to you every night since you were taken...

I see the moon, and the moon sees me
The moon sees the one that I want to see
So, God bless the moon and God bless me and
God bless the one that I want to see

I love you my sweet Tessa, my sweet daughter.

Love,
Momma

Too stunned to respond or react in anyway, Tessa carefully re-read her mother's words. She read them out loud, slowly and carefully. She was thrown off kilter, certainly, but her skills as an attorney, her ability to read tough documents without emotion helped her try and wade through the words and find the truth. When she had lost count of how many times she had read them, her questions could be silenced no longer. The letter didn't make sense. Caroline spoke as though Tessa had been adopted, as if she were gone and Caroline would never see her again. How could that be? Tessa had never been told she had been adopted, it was never mentioned. As far as she knew she had been with Marian and Henry her entire life. If she had been adopted, if Caroline believed she was gone, how had she come back home? Had her father not walked away like Henry said? It was too much, none of it made sense. The words and questions spiraled into a kaleidoscope, brilliant colors and patterns with no answers. Tessa's mind narrowed in on the words she had waited a lifetime to feel: *I love you my sweet Tessa. I love you my sweet Tessa.*

The questions stepped away. The wondering faded. The confusion was silenced by sweet salvation as Tessa reveled in the knowledge that her mother *loved her*. In this moment the only thing that mattered was that the truth that Tessa had ached for her entire life was real. It was vibrant and alive with the words of her mother echoing in her mind. *I love you my sweet Tessa.*

The belief she had built her life on, the foundation that she was not worthy of love and forgiveness cracked. Tomorrow she would worry about how she came to be Marian and Henry's daughter, how her mother had come to believe her daughter had been taken, how any of this happened. For now, that was all she needed to know was that her mother loved her.

Tess's tears fell, blending with the ink on the letter her mother had written her before she took her own life. Mother and daughter, their sadness pooling together over words that had waited twenty-eight years to be read. In all the ways that Tess had defined herself in this life — daughter to a gypsy hippy, granddaughter to Henry, granddaughter to Marian, lawyer, lover, friend — none of them have ever defined her as strongly as: daughter of a mother who did not stay. Sarah Beth had been right,

Caroline didn't leave this earth embarrassed and ashamed of Tessa's existence. She left this world heartbroken that her daughter would be someone else's to raise. *My mother loved me. My mother loved me. My mother loved me.* The sadness of all she had lost overwhelmed Tess, like the icy May water of the lake.

Hot bile rose in Tess's throat. The foundation that Tess's life was built on crumbled, and a new, sturdier bedrock began to take its place. Beads of sweat collected on her brow and on the nape of her neck. Deep inside her body, the truth of her mother's love thrashed away at the lies that Tess had always believed. The heaviness broke apart in serrated pieces, and Tessa began to tremble. The warmth of her mother's love began to thaw her heart from the inside out. Tess rocked back and forth. All Tess had wanted since she was a little girl was to be someone's first choice. Their person. The one they loved above all else. She was first to her mother, it was what she always wanted. The reality of it was incredibly bittersweet. To be the one your mother loved above all else would have been all she had needed, if her mother had only been there to see it through.

Tessa began to wail. She cried from deep inside her gut. She tried to read her mother's letter again, but her tears blurred the words, leaving Tessa with her thoughts. How sad, how very tragic. Henry lost his daughter, Caroline lost her mother, and yes, Marian lost her daughter too. It didn't have to be that way. Grief continued to shake Tessa, her tears and shaking in concert released the sadness she had carried with her all her life.

She expected a torrent of anger. She waited to feel the bitterness of regret, to feel the hot madness she has shouldered for Marian to explode.

It didn't come. Instead, forgiveness settled in her heart. Marian did the best she could. Tess had never seen Marian as Caroline's mother, as someone who had suffered an unspeakable loss. She had only seen what Marian withheld from her — warmth, nurturing, compassion. Only now can she see what Caroline's death stole from Marian. She had given Tessa all she had. She gave her what she could: structure, discipline, dependability. What Tessa saw as ill will was Marian trying to survive, trying to survive the greatest heartache a mother can hold.

There was knocking on the door, but Tessa ignored the sound. She barely registered the noise as something to act upon. The knocking continued, and then faded for a bit. Tessa put the letter back in its envelope and tucked it into her purse. It was too hard to hold. She climbed back under the covers of her bed and sobbed. She sobbed hard enough she didn't hear the door open, or see Davis as he came to her side.

"Tessa, baby I'm right here," Davis whispered as he reached out to touch her. He was careful, expecting her to flinch at the brush of his fingers on her arm. "I've got you," he says. "I've got you."

He came to love her.

And after all this time, she let him.

Chapter Twenty

Tessa started at the beginning. She told Davis about Roger Lanford, showed him the newspaper with Marian's obituary from Joe to Go, Grandpa Henry's copy of *Pride and Prejudice* that she had taken her first day back at Front Street, the photograph of young Caroline in dirty white shoes and her mother's letter. She told him about her imaginary hippy mother, the death certificate and the fight with Marian, and Sarah Beth and Jimmy, Zoe and Maddy and Elizabeth. Tessa told Davis about them all. She laid her life out in an offering to him and he softly took it in his hands and listened.

Shortly before dawn, after Tessa had cried and talked and held onto Davis for hours, he touched her cheek with the back of his hand. She held his hand in her own, warmed by his compassion and understanding, his willingness to forgive her for nearly ending their relationship, for running away. She wept as they made love, the light of the sun warming the room with purple and green gladiolas on the bedspread, the room where Tessa had lost and found herself; the room where Tessa finally gave herself — her past and her future — to Davis, in room 111 of the Waterside Inn in Chapel Corners.

The pair slept soundly until after noon, holding on to

the truth and each other. Reenie had left homemade cinnamon bread, apples and bananas outside their door. They ate at the table facing the sliver view of the lake.

"I just can't believe you're here," Tessa said.

Davis smiled. "I feel like we've been on a pilgrimage back to 1989 and back. It feels like I've been here your whole life."

"In the last ten years, I never imagined coming back, ever again. Here I am sitting in the Waterside Inn with you." Davis leaned forward and kissed Tess's forehead. "Thank you for coming after me. I don't think I deserved it."

"The thing about that is, you don't get to tell me what you deserve from me," his eyes were somber. "Honestly... I wasn't sure I was going to come. I was pretty angry after you left Saturday night," Davis said honestly.

"I know I let you down. I was so afraid. When I got the call from Roger Lanford Saturday afternoon, it got under my skin. I just ran." Tessa looked away from Davis's gaze. "What made you decide to come?"

"Adrianna was the one who pushed me. I'd given up, honestly. I had called, you didn't answer. You weren't reaching out to me. She showed up in my office, busted into the middle of a meeting with Ryan."

"She did not." Tessa smiled thinking of Adrianna from A's Couture waltzing into Renford Construction like she owned the place.

"Oh she did. She's a piece of work, that one."

"Adrianna has been good to me over the years, but I

don't think we have ever been real friends. I think we served a common purpose… she likes to think, talk, and be about herself and I didn't want anything to be about me. Perfect fit."

"She was worried about you, in her own A's Couture way." Davis laughed as he pulled Tessa toward him. "As much as I hate to admit it, she's a better friend to you than I gave her credit for."

"Oh, I know that… I really do. I know she loves me in the best way she can, but I think I need more than just that now. I need to give a piece of myself, too."

"I'll take a piece."

"You can have the biggest piece." Tess leaned forward, stretching her neck to touch him gently on the lips. "Let's go for a walk, I want to show you something."

. . . .

The sun was high in the sky now, peeking through dark bands of clouds. Rain was coming. They quietly walked hand in hand down toward the water. Tessa held two Waterside Inn towels under her arm. After they picked a spot on the beach, she spread out the towels in the sand before she plunked herself down pulling Davis with her. "Do you think the lake is different from this side?" Tess asked, snuggling into the crook of Davis's outstretched arm.

"It's peaceful here… the water seems bigger from this side for some reason," he answered.

"I felt it the minute I pulled into town, even though I

was nervous as hell to come back here. The slowness of it compared to Chicago speaks to me."

Davis nodded his head in answer.

"I went to the cemetery the other night, before I found my mom's letter." Tessa stared evenly at the horizon. "I went to tell my grandpa that I was okay, that I knew what happened and I was sorry that I left without saying goodbye. I saw my mom's grave and do you know what bothered me the most?" Davis tilted his head, listening. "Besides the fact that I had never seen it before, it really got me that her gravestone said 'Loving daughter.' That's it, nothing about being my mother, nothing connecting the two of us." Tessa's eyes filled with tears again. "I can't stop crying. I haven't cried in ten years and now I can't stop."

Davis smiled sadly. "I'm sorry, baby."

"Don't be sorry. It's good crying. It's a lot of years of hiding and pretending that I'm getting out from behind." Tessa took in a deep breath of the lake air and closed her eyes. "You love me, don't you?" she asked him.

"You can't tell?" Davis smiled and pulled Tessa down to kiss her head. "Yes, I love you, Tessa Wallace."

Tessa let him kiss her and then looked back up to see the horizon. "Where do you think people go when they die?"

"I don't think I ever *thought* about it… I was taught that we go to heaven and I don't think I ever challenged that," Davis answered.

"Hmm…" Tessa nodded her head as she watched the waves roll up on the sand. The sun was still in her eyes as it poked in and out of clouds, she squinted and smiled. "I feel Henry here. I always have. Whenever I am by the water I can feel him. Not a creepy 'he's watching my every move' kinda way, I just feel him. I can feel him giving me energy. I feel the knowledge of him and his life, what he believed and loved. He loved me, and at times in my life it felt like he was the only one who ever did."

"He's not, he wasn't," Davis answered. The sun gave way to small, gentle rain drops. "Do you know what this reminds me of?"

"Jaco Beach," she answered without hesitation. "I was thinking about that trip earlier this week."

"I will never forget watching you surf that day. You smiled from ear to ear." Davis laughed.

"And the fish tacos!" Tessa smiled. "I never wanted to leave. I *was* so happy that day. I felt like the real me. Chapel Corners, Marian, Henry, my mom. They were all so far away I felt like they couldn't touch me. I felt like I could just be the me I always wanted to be, without all that baggage. Funny thing is, I was still thinking about it. I wasn't free of it like I wanted to be."

Davis lay back on his towel, letting the sprinkling rain land on his cool skin. He had waited so long for Tessa to open up and let him in, he was careful to listen, not talk.

"This is so much better. This is me, this is what I am, who I am. Some of it isn't very pretty."

"We all have those stories, Tessa," Davis answered quietly. He pulled her down into the crook of his arm and nestled her up against him as the rain fell. Baptizing them all over again.

Chapter Twenty-One

Davis and Tessa sat inside his BMW as they waited for Roger Lanford to arrive at his office. The daffodils that had lined the sidewalk brilliantly just a few days ago now showed the slightest signs of wilting with limp petals and faded color. The tulips behind them reached up toward the sun, blooms at the ready when the warmth and sun and water were right. *Life changes,* Tessa thought, *right before your eyes.* She squeezed Davis's hand, thankful to have him with her. Fear bolted from Tess's eyes. Davis leaned into her body, touching her shoulder across the cool leather. He kissed her neck tenderly.

"You ready?" he asked. Tessa drummed her fingers on the sides of the seat, looking out at the house. She rolled the window up and down several times, adjusting her temperature. The warm, subtle breezes of the past week were gone; a cold front had swept in with the rain and clouds hung low overhead. Late spring had returned to Michigan.

"I think I am," Tessa answered. Lanford's headlights lit up the inside of the BMW as he pulled up into the drive. Tessa and Davis got out of the car and waited for him on the steps.

"I'm sorry, folks. Hope I didn't keep you waiting too long." The tired old man craned his body out of his worn

Chevy truck, using the handle on the door for assistance. He shuffled slowly in front of them as they followed him up the walk toward the old blue house. The Christmas lights that were hanging from the eves were gone and the porch had been swept. New baskets of flowers adorned the doorway on either side, guests were now greeted by purple pansies. Roger let them both in as he held open the door. Tessa and Davis stopped just inside the front room waiting for Roger to lead the way.

"Thanks so much for seeing us on a Friday night like this," Tessa said.

"That's quite all right, I got the idea it was important." Roger smiled, his eyes gentle.

"Roger, this is Davis Renford. Davis, Roger Lanford." Tess's stomach twisted and turned as the two men exchanged pleasantries. She rocked back and forth from heels to toes as she waited. A chilly breeze hung in the air from the still-open door. Tess looked hard at the flowers, the grass, and the trees, knowing that what she learned in the next hour may change how she looked at all those things. The open door was a portal into her past, and where she stood was the entrance to her future and the truth. Even though she had most of the pieces now, she had learned not to take anything for granted. If there was anything new Roger could tell her, it had the power to change how she looked at her family, and she was not sure she could take that again so soon.

Roger led Tessa and Davis back through the kitchenette and conference room toward his office in the rear of the old house. Tessa held Davis's hand as they navigated their way through the towering piles of files and found two chairs opposing Roger's desk. Davis took a stack of papers off of the second chair, crossing his legs at the knee and ankle, sitting back quietly. He was here to support Tessa, this was not his meeting. Tessa sat perched on the edge of her seat, feet tucked under her and crossed while she leaned even farther forward onto her palms. Roger methodically took off his jacket, stowed his keys in the top drawer on the left-hand side, pulled his pants up slightly before sitting down and laced his fingers together leaning forward on his desk.

"What can I do for you, Tessa? I assume that this is not about the renunciation papers for Marian's will." Roger cleared his throat and waited.

"You're right, it's not. Thank you though, for doing that work for me. I do appreciate it. I came across some information while I was cleaning out Marian's house and I am hoping you can fill in the gaps?" Tess's voice lilted upward at the end of her thought.

Roger Lanford settled back in his chair, bringing his elbows with him to respite on the arm rest of his chair. Tessa paused, closed her eyes and pulled in a long breath.

"I had always been told as a child that my mother, Caroline, died giving birth to me. Shortly before I left Chapel Corners I discovered that she actually had committed suicide." Tessa wiped her now-sweaty palms across her jeans and clasped them together in her lap. Roger continued to listen, nodding and patiently waiting for Tessa to continue.

"I discovered a letter my mother wrote to me while

cleaning out the house. It's given me a lot of peace." Tessa took a deep breath and reached for Davis's hand. "It's also given me a lot of questions." Tessa reached down into her purse and pulled the letter out of her purse handing it to Roger. "I'm hoping that you can help me understand the rest of the story. My story." Tessa's eyes were rimmed with tears.

Roger took the letter with care, gingerly opening and reading quietly. When he was done, he took his glasses off and wiped tears from his eyes. Tessa sat with Davis, holding his hand and waiting.

"Your mother was a beautiful young woman, bright-eyed and smart. And feisty." Roger laughed a little as his hands fell unclasped into his lap. "Marian was furious with her for getting pregnant so young, and unmarried. Henry's heart was broken; she was the apple of his eye... much like you. They sent her to Sister Mary Teresa's, a convent by the ocean in New Hampshire. Marian insisted. Henry tried to change her mind but Marian was stubborn. She felt she was protecting Caroline's future. She didn't think Caroline was old enough to be a mother. She stayed in New Hampshire for the remainder of her pregnancy, and your birth."

Tessa's eyes blinked rapidly. She had always believed she was born in Michigan. Davis continued to hold Tess's hand as she rocked back and forth in her chair.

"Marian came to me and asked me to draw up papers to terminate Caroline's parental rights and then place the baby — you — up for adoption. I was concerned, not having spoken with Caroline herself. But Marian and I had known each other since we were kids, as I told you before, and she was insistent that this was what Caroline wanted. It wasn't until after her death that Henry came to me and I learned Marian had lied. Caroline had not willingly agreed to the adoption. Marian had strong-armed her, Caroline was isolated in the convent and I'm sure felt she had no way out. Marian could be fierce and Caroline was young and completely dependent on her parents.

"I knew Marian for most of my life. She had a very difficult childhood. Her father was an abusive alcoholic. She was the oldest of seven kids, and much of the care and safety of her siblings fell to her. When she met Henry, she escaped her father, but she never got over the pain of her childhood. Now I know that she wasn't the easiest person to live with and be raised by, but she did the best she could. She learned how to protect herself when she was young, and even the love of Henry and Caroline was not enough to soften her heart." Roger stopped, waiting for Tess to nod her approval to continue.

"After your birth, your mom was allowed to keep you for a few days. In hindsight, that may have been too much for Caroline. She fell into a depression. The nuns tried to help. They fed her, bathed her, prayed with her. It wasn't enough. Caroline must have saved the pain medication they gave her, and took it all at once. She hung on for a few days. Long enough for Marian and Henry to get there to say goodbye. It was after her passing that Henry asked the nuns if they could rescind the adoption. I was the only one who knew where

Caroline had been sent. Your Grandpa Henry called to tell me what happened and ask for legal advice. You were only three weeks old. Typically a newborn would have been adopted by then, but you were sick and hospitalized with pneumonia. Because of the circumstances surrounding your mother's death and, frankly, the adoptive parents were concerned about adopting a baby who already had health issues, the nuns at St. Teresa's were very willing to work with us to bring you back to Henry and Marian."

"So you brought me back."

"I helped facilitate the legal papers to bring you back. Your Grandpa Henry brought you back."

"Marian didn't want me, did she?" Tessa asked.

"After Caroline died, Marian was never the same. The guilt and grief ate away at her. I don't think it was as much that she didn't want you as she wanted her daughter back. And in her mind, it was an either or. She couldn't have you both."

Tessa held her head in her hands and began to cry. So much of what had happened to her she didn't understand. She had spent a lifetime trying to make Marian happy. She had spent a lifetime missing her mother, and the last decade hating Marian and believing she was not enough. Davis wrapped his arm around her shoulder as she cried. The comfort he provided was foreign, but welcome. It felt good to not do things on her own, to have support when she needed it, to be real and be honest.

"Why did Marian make me the executor of her will?" Tessa asked through tears, reaching for a Kleenex off

Lanford's desk.

"I can tell you that Marian knew her health was failing. The last time we had dinner she discussed a desire to cleanse her past, to let it go. I wonder now if she knew how little time she had left," Roger questioned. "When she came to me to arrange for the changes to her will that provided for you and the Children's Action Organization, I questioned her about her choice. I knew you had been estranged and I wasn't sure you would want to accept the responsibilities. She believed you would come home and take care of things. She was positive you would. She wanted you to come. She wanted you to have Henry's things, and now I see that she also wanted you to find the letter."

"And I did." Tessa was stunned that the woman she thought didn't know her at all had predicted exactly what she would do.

"She made a lot of mistakes, Tessa, and she knew that. When Caroline became pregnant, she went into survival mode. She wanted to save her daughter's future. Marian always wanted to go to college, she never got the chance because she was taking care of all of her siblings. She wanted more for Caroline, in her mind the only way for her daughter's future to be salvaged was for you to be adopted. Knowing she made the decision that caused her daughter to take her own life was not something she could handle. She threw herself into raising you the best that she could with who she had become after she lost Caroline.

"Tessa, please understand, I am in no way justifying

her actions, I am just trying to give you the full picture. She was a damaged woman, and without her own version of the truth, what she did to Caroline would have killed her. In reality, it probably did." Roger Lanford leaned forward in his chair, hanging his head slightly. "For nearly twenty-eight years my part in this story has weighed on my mind. I have never, nor will I ever, forgive myself for simply taking your grandmother's word as Caroline's. I owe you an apology, and I know that isn't good enough, but it's all I have. I am very sorry."

Tessa stood and reached for Roger's hand across his desk. "You trusted Marian. You couldn't have known. In a strange twist of fate, you have also given me a gift. You gave me the gift of the truth, and the truth has given me a new way of looking at things. I am so grateful for that."

Roger Lanford hung his head in humble acceptance. "Your mother would be so proud of the woman you have become."

"And now, it's time for me to be proud of the woman I am." Tessa picked up the envelope holding her mother's letter, held onto Davis's hand and walked out of Lanford and Associates.

....

Tessa sat alone on the kitchen floor of her childhood home. The clock no longer hung on the wall, the chairs hugged the bare dining room table and the cupboards were empty. The house was dark and quiet. Three days ago Tessa would have refused to stay in this room this way. Tonight, it was exactly what she needed.

After Tessa and Davis left Lanford's office they had gone for a drive down by the lake and circled through town. Tessa showed Davis her high school and McGinney's Orchard. It had been dark, but Tessa had wanted to offer more of herself. She had wanted to show him the other side of Chapel Corners, the side that had nurtured and cared for her as she had grown up. They grabbed a late coffee at Cup of Joe and Tessa asked him to drop her off at Front Street. It was time for her to say goodbye, and she needed to do that alone.

She rummaged through the boxes she and Sarah Beth had left lined up against the wall. Finding what she needed, she struck the match and lit the lone taper candle she could find. Marian deserved a service, even if it was just Tessa.

In the dark of the kitchen, Tessa sat cross-legged on the floor. She wasn't sure what she would do to honor her grandmother, so she sat and waited for the right words to come. Holding the candle in vigil with both her hands in front of her chest, she closed her eyes and said The Lord's Prayer. Then she began to sing *Amazing Grace*, her mind remembering all the words to the first verse flawlessly. Her voice was strong, it carried with it forgiveness and love. She could see her grandmother standing in the church choir in front of the congregation, navy-blue choir robe pressed perfectly, her hair in a flawless bun, nothing out of place. Her strong jaw and forehead giving the illusion of control, when Tessa knew now how deeply wounded Marian was. Life had not been kind to her grandmother. Tessa felt the words of the song wash over her. She wept at the relief the forgiveness she held gave her. For Henry, for Caroline, for Marian and for herself. They had done the best they could.

Amazing grace! How sweet the sound
That saved a wretch like me!
I once was lost, but now am found;
Was blind, but now I see.

When she was done singing, she knew, without a doubt, what she needed to say to the woman who had raised her, who had stepped in as a mother when she needed one. To the woman who had eluded her, who had largely ignored and pained her, who had also cared for and hurt her. Tessa needed to offer forgiveness, and ask for forgiveness herself.

"I have spent my life hiding from my past. I pretended to be someone I'm not, I couldn't let anyone in." Tessa took a deep, jagged breath. "I blamed you for that for most of my life. I decided my past, you, Henry, my mom, our story was all too awful to share. I believed that if anyone really knew who I was and how I came to be in this world they would walk away. No questions asked.

"I was wrong. It's not too awful. I'm not going to pretend that you and I were close, or romanticize how it really was. It wasn't good, and I wouldn't want any child to grow up feeling as lonely and sad as I did. What I have now is understanding. What I have now is forgiveness."

Tessa's eyes began to swell with tears. Her voice was deep with emotion.

"I forgive you. I forgive you so that the tragic story of Caroline Wallace can come to an end. I forgive you so that my mother can rest in peace. I forgive you so that my Grandpa Henry can rest in peace. I forgive you so that *you* can rest in peace. And maybe most importantly, I forgive you so that *I* can have peace. I want peace and I want a future. A future that is about all of me, not just what I think is good enough for people to see.

"I understand now, as I never did then, how hard it was for you to step in and be my mother. I don't know what it feels like to lose a child, and I pray I never do. What I do know is that I never offered you any empathy or compassion for losing Caroline. I regret that, I'm so sorry for that. I wonder now if I had offered the slightest bit of understanding, of caring that you had lost her too, how that might have changed us."

Tessa stood and began to walk around the small home. The soft light from the candle cast gentle shadows on the walls. The sadness and loneliness Tessa felt here faded. It was not what defined her. She realized that the past could be a part of her history, that it could contribute to who she is — a driven, focused woman, a woman who has been hurt, a woman who wants to give more of who she is — but it did not have to define her for life. The realization was liberating. When Tessa opened the door to self-acceptance, forgiveness stepped in.

As difficult as it was for Tessa to return to Chapel

Corners, as much as she did not want to be the executor of Marian's estate or clean out the house or tell Davis the truth, she couldn't deny that she would not have a future that included Davis and Sarah Beth and Adri and her truth without those things. By naming Tessa the executor of her will, Marian had set into motion a plan to bring Tess closure, to bring her the truth and a chance at true happiness. Marian knew she would come home.

And she had.

Chapter Twenty-Two

Tessa took one last amble around the backyard at Front Street. The ferns in the back of the house by the old mulberry tree were stronger now, unfurling their frail leaves fully into the spring. The house had been cleared of all of Henry's belongings, as well as what was left that was Caroline's. Davis had arranged for movers to transfer what would be going to a storage unit in Chicago and what would be boxed and taken to Volunteers of America. The playhouse would go to Sarah Beth and Jimmy's tomorrow; Tessa's chest lifted higher when she thought of the two sisters playing inside the lonely walls, bringing them back to life as she and Sarah Beth had.

The grass was moist with evening dew. The temperature was still cooler than it had been for the last week, leaving a blue mist in the air. Everything felt different here now. The steel veil that had been draped over Chapel Corners in her memory was fading, even the grass at her feet felt new. Her mother had played here, run barefoot and laughed, sang songs and ate ice cream. The thought both saddened and comforted her. Tessa slid her feet closer to the earth, digging her toes into the connection with her mother.

Davis was packing the two cars now parked in the driveway with a few of the items Tessa had wanted to take with her, mainly Henry's books and some of Caroline's clothes and pictures. Sarah Beth and Jimmy had come and gone, leaving behind them a new wake of sadness. Promises were made to write and call — and even visit. Tessa took with her pictures of Zoe and Maddy, and one of Sarah Beth and Tessa that Mrs. McGinney had saved from high school. Tessa had tucked it on the visor of her car. She needed the physical reminder of the connections she had made, the hope she felt and the warmth of friendship. Both women had cried. It had been the goodbye they had deserved ten years ago, and a new beginning to a friendship Tessa hoped would carry them into their futures.

"Hey babe, there's someone here to see you," Davis called to Tessa from the front of the house. Tessa walked up to the patio doors. Slipping her shoes back on her feet, she walked through the house to the front door.

A man stood at the end of the sidewalk wearing a navy-blue zip-up jacket with a white collared shirt peeking over the cuff. He was tall and had sandy hair salted with gray; his jaw was strong, holding a deep cleft. His eyes were kind and pleading. A worry pooled there that she noticed now was spread out through his sturdy build. The sun was bright, peering down like a spotlight. Their eyes connected, and all at once Tessa knew. She knew why her grandfather took her on weekly trips for ice cream to Castle Pharmacy. She knew why Luke Castle jumped in to save her from the icy water. Today the sun's rays hit his eyes in just the way that Tessa could see the same honey-colored ring embedded in the emerald green that she saw in the mirror every day. He was her mother's Luke.

He was her father.

"Reenie came by the store to tell me you were leaving town. I hope it's okay that I stopped to see you off." Luke's hands fidgeted deep inside his pockets, his fingers rolling in anticipation and worry.

"Sure." Tessa took one hesitant step toward him, shutting the door to Front Street behind her. Their eyes pulled them together as Tessa's breath became shallow and ragged. All her life she had focused on her mother, imagining and dreaming of who she would have been, wondering how a relationship with her mother would have felt. She had never fantasized about who her father was. She had Henry, he had filled that ache before it began. Looking into the eyes of her father, she knew now that what she needed, had always needed, was to look into the eyes of where she came from.

"I'm sorry, Tessa." Luke's hands fell out of his pockets. Helpless to defend his absence or answer her forthcoming questions, he simply held his hands out to her.

Taking his hands in her own, Tessa could feel the aged skin beneath her fingertips. The years she had missed being warm and shielded by those hands stood silently around her. "Is it you?" Their hands squeezed together as Luke nodded his head, tears puddled in his eyes and his shoulders began to shake.

"I'm your father." Luke held his head up, his chest rising with the breath he took from their shared space. Davis had been lingering near the cars, giving Tessa liberty to conduct her own business. Now he stepped forward beside Luke and Tessa.

"Davis, this is Luke Castle." Tessa paused as their hands remained together. "He's my father." The two men exchanged nods as Tessa and Luke continued holding onto each other; so many years had slipped past them. All her life she had been an orphan, now suddenly she was someone's daughter.

Davis suggested they go for a walk while he finished up at the house. Tessa and Luke walked side by side, not speaking for a while, giving each other space to gather the courage needed to go on. Tessa watched the houses of her familiar neighborhood pass by. Some were different, renovated and updated, some sold and others stayed richly the same. Since she had arrived in Chapel Corners the way she viewed the world was different with each new piece of information. Nothing looked the same, and nothing was different.

"I loved your mother," Luke started. "We wanted to get married, we tried to keep the pregnancy a secret until after we graduated. We really thought that if we waited until then, our parents couldn't do anything about it."

Tessa nodded, looking straight ahead as she listened. Her feelings draped across her shoulders like a heavy coat. She thought to tell Luke about the letter, but hesitated. She wanted to hear the truth from him. She wanted to know how he saw the past.

"Your grandmother found out, I never really knew how. Everything happened very quickly. Caroline was gone in a matter of days after her pregnancy was discovered and I... I never saw her again."

It suddenly occurred to Tessa that Luke was probably never told the truth about how Caroline died. The truth of how their family was destroyed had started a profound change in Tessa over the last few days. She was still unsure how she felt about what she now knew. Should she tell Luke?

"I tried to communicate with her, I wrote her, and tried to call... but all of my attempts were refused. It was terrible. I did everything I could to prove that we would make it as a family. I got a job, saved money and even looked for apartments to rent in Covington." Luke took a deep breath before continuing. "You know I don't even know your exact birthday?" Luke shook his head, dismayed at the past and his part in what brought them to this moment.

"September third, 1977," Tess answered.

"Hmm... you were due on the seventh. No one called me when you were born. They didn't call me when Caroline died."

"Luke, do you know how she died?" Tessa bit at her lip, her stomach hollowed out like a cavern. What she chose to share with her father would forever change him. This would hurt. The past week she learned that sharing the truth with those you love is the only way to a real connection.

"When Henry came home, he came to see me. He told me that she had suffered complications with your birth and didn't make it. I was so young, and very much in love with your mother, I didn't even understand that women *could* die during childbirth. I didn't ask any questions, I didn't know what *to* ask. In my heart of hearts I always believed she died from a broken heart." Luke took a long slow breath, tipping his head up toward the heavens. "She wanted you, Tessa. She wanted you more than anything. You were a surprise to both of us, but we loved each other and we loved you. We were young and certainly naive, but we wanted a life together. Taking her away from me the way they did, away from her home, cutting her off from her friends and school, would have been survivable; losing you never would have been. The longer she stayed gone, the clearer it became to me that I probably would never hold you, and neither would Caroline." The two had reached a park at the end of the road, empty today now that the chilly temperatures and patches of cloudy skies had returned.

Tessa and Luke were quiet as they walked to an empty swing set. They sat in a pair of swings, the black vinyl chilled Tessa's legs through her jeans. The chains suspending the swing from the steel bar were cold and chunky in her hands.

"We used to come to this park, your mom and me. After we found out she was expecting you, we came nearly every day. We could talk out loud together without being afraid of getting caught." Tessa dragged her feet slowly back and forth in the sandy pit beneath the swing. A woman bundled in a heavy spring jacket and a stocking cap pulled down over her head walked by pushing a stroller cradling a pudgy baby with pink cheeks and peaceful, drowsy eyes. The woman smiled at Luke and

Tessa, Tessa smiled back and began.

"Luke, she killed herself." The words tumbled out of her mouth quicker than she would have liked. Tessa felt the swing swallowing her. She stared straight ahead, listening to the silence. The blood rushed in her ears, making her hot and uncomfortable. "I didn't know until I was a teenager, that's why I left Chapel Corners. You were right, she did die of a broken heart."

Luke held his face in his hands and wept, the nippy breeze stinging the salty tears to his skin. Tessa gently pushed herself back and forth before going on and telling her father of the fight she had with Marian all those years ago, the letter she found and her visit with Roger Lanford. Through it all Luke stayed still, absorbing the story of his lost family. When Tessa was done speaking, they returned to the silence of the park. A few optimistic birds sang out to them, a few stray leaves rustled by in the breeze. Time and space stood still.

"I remember the first time I saw you. Your grandpa Henry brought you into the store when you were just a few weeks old. You were so little, frail and delicate, and you looked just like Caroline. You still do. I saw her every time I looked in your eyes. It broke my heart."

"Why didn't anyone tell me who you were? I mean obviously I was too little then, but what about later? When I was older?" Tessa asked.

"Henry promised to bring you to the pharmacy for regular visits if I promised to not tell you I was your dad." Luke shook his head. "I was so young. I did what I thought was right, I didn't believe I could raise you

213

alone."

"Grandpa Henry did?" Tessa felt a hot flash of anger toward Henry. She had trusted him her entire life, she had idolized him. He was the best man she knew. How could he keep the truth from her about something so important?

"Tessa, if I was heartbroken after Caroline died, Henry nearly died himself. He and Caroline were so close, and when he lost her it nearly killed him. You were what saved him, kept him moving. And I was eighteen years old, I had deferred college for one semester in anticipation of your mom and you returning – it seems selfish now, but at the time I didn't believe in my ability to take care of you. I let Henry have you, and I kept my time to weekly visits for ice cream. I took the sure thing. I was broken without Caroline, I didn't think I could do it without her." Luke defended Henry and Tessa felt her heart soften.

"We all do the best we can, that's all we can ask of anybody," Tessa answered quietly.

"When you left town I tried tracking you down. I wanted to tell you everything. By the time I found you, you were living in Chicago, going to school. I told myself you were happy. I didn't know what good would come of my interfering. I was afraid. If I kept you where I could see you and watch over you, then I would never have to hear you tell me to go away or that you hated me. If I kept you from the truth then you could never not be mine. I don't know if you can understand that..." Luke's words bled into a whisper.

"I think I do. After Marian told me how Caroline died, I was determined I would carve out my own place in this world away from Chapel Corners, Marian and my mother. I wanted peace; I wanted to stop hearing the voice in my head that kept telling me I wasn't even worth my own mother staying with me." Tessa looked up at the bars that held the suspended swings. "Davis has helped me to see that I can decide how to define myself, I can decide my worth and I don't have to leave that in the hands of my past, or my enemies, or even my friends. I define me. Not my mother's suicide, or your decision to let Henry and Marian raise me. Not Henry's omissions or Marian's neglect. This story, my past, is just a part of my journey. It only has an impact on what my future is if I allow it. I always thought I didn't want it to affect me at all. I mean, that's why I left here, right? To start over, make a new life." Luke bowed his head, indicating that he understood.

"What I learned this week is that I can choose to take the good parts, grow them and build off of them. The love Henry gave me, Sarah Beth's friendship, weekly visits for ice cream, and yes, even the years I spent with Marian as a mother. She raised me the best she could, all while sheltering the greatest pain a mother can hold deep inside her heart. I always thought there was something wrong with me, that I was just not good enough, lovable or worth her time. The truth is that Marian was broken. Caroline's death — and the role Marian played in it — broke her. She gave me all she had to give and tried to protect me from a very painful truth. That's all you can ask of anyone." Tessa nodded her head, letting Luke know she was done.

"I am sorry. I'm sorry you have lost so much. I weighed very carefully the risk I put you in by telling you I am your dad. In life I have learned that the truth shouldn't always be shared. Your intention has to be true. Sharing the truth to rid yourself of guilt or to lessen your own burden can be hurtful. Sharing your truth with others so that they can lean in to you, so that they better understand themselves, is a gift. The greater gift must be *given* by speaking the truth, not received. In the end, I decided that I could tell you things about your mother that no one else can. I can share with you parts of her that only I knew. That, after all these years, is my gift to both of you." Luke began to weep in the way that only a lifetime of sadness and regret brings. "I should have saved you."

"Ahh... but I learned how to save myself," Tessa answered.

"You are just like your mother." Luke continued to weep soft, gentle tears as Tessa smiled, soaking in the warmth of her father's love after a lifetime of separation.

"Luke, will you do me a favor?"

"Anything for my daughter," Luke replied.

"Push me?" Tessa smiled.

If she stretched her legs as long as she could, Tessa's toes poked up over the canopy of the trees at the park. The sun had begun its descent into another day on the other side of the world. Air rushed far into her chest, pushing stale oxygen from the deep pockets of her lungs, sending vibrant, intense signals to her body. Tessa was awake and as real as the chilly air that cleansed her spirit. She felt her father's strong, unfamiliar hands on her back, pushing her farther and farther into the sky, up to where her spirit was free and light and her body left the seat of the swing for a moment. The awkward chains of the swing held loosely in her hands made her smile. She was finally at peace with her past and her life. Marian, Henry, Caroline and Luke had all made choices that affected Tessa. Today, nestled in the safety of a swing, high atop the ground, she knew she had made choices, too. She had chosen to run away, she left Sarah Beth and their friendship, she had held Davis and Adrianna at a distance, she had even walked away from Mark, all in an effort to keep her past hidden, to be someone else, to not have to face some ugly truths. Tessa had allowed her past to define her, when all along all she had to do was to decide for herself. Decide to accept her mother and grandparents where they were. Accept that they did what they could, and so did she.

Her father's hands pushed one more time across her back, launching Tessa straight up in the air. This time she let go of the gawky chains, slipped her body out of the cradle of the swing and jumped solo into the future, feeling finally, fiercely alive.

Epilogue

The snow is already six inches deep and continues to fall. We are back in Chapel Corners to visit with my dad and his wife, Cynthia, and of course Sarah Beth, Jimmy and the girls, for Christmas.

Life has taken some twists and turns. I'm still learning to let Davis in, and Davis is still patient with me. It's hard to uproot patterns you've always had, but I try every day. We are both searching for that work-life balance. I am taking Stan Epstein's yoga class three mornings a week, and every Sunday night Davis and I sit on his balcony — rain, shine or snow — and watch the sunset. I would still like to make partner, but if it doesn't happen, I'll be all right.

Lucy and I eat lunch together once a week. I have even babysat for her daughter Emma a few times while she goes out on dates with James, her new beau. Adrianna is still dramatic and self-centered, but I have also learned she's a pretty good listener when someone actually has something to say. Sarah Beth and I talk about once a week. I FaceTime the girls and we text quite a bit. There is such comfort and peace in having someone in your life that has known you from the beginning, who understands your story and loves you anyway. I wish I hadn't wasted so much time, but it is what it is. Along with forgiving

Caroline, Henry and Marian, I am learning to forgive myself. I do the best I can.

We pull into the parking lot and I am surprised by where we are. I look out the window and see my dad and Cynthia standing outside in the cold. Cynthia is a warm, engaging woman who has accepted me into her life, home and family. It's a new experience for me to have a mother figure who is so attentive and kind. She treads carefully and slowly, I appreciate that. The snow has begun piling up on their coats and hats. My dad smiles at me, Cynthia waves. Sarah Beth and Jimmy are quiet in the back seat and Davis smiles at me as he turns off the engine to the BMW.

"What are we doing here?" I ask.

No one will answer me, they just get out of the car and shut their doors behind them. I pull on my gloves and follow them outside. The snow is falling harder now, it's beautiful and quiet. A pretty white blanket covers the cemetery. It is tucked in for the winter. The roll of the surf in the distance is the only sound, it brings me comfort.

"Dad, I thought we were meeting at the restaurant?" He and Cynthia are standing by the open gate toward the cemetery.

"Hi, sweetheart," my dad says. "Your fiancé had a change of plans." A kiss comes to my cheek from his warm, soft lips, his scratchy cheeks graze my skin and it feels good, fatherly. Cynthia leans in, taking her gloved hand to stroke my cheek where she has left a damp kiss as well.

Davis comes around the back of the car with a long white floral box, handing it to me ceremoniously. Inside there are a dozen beautiful white roses and a card that reads:

The white roses symbolize respect, honors new starts and hope for the future. I think they are perfect for today. All my love, Adrianna.

I slip the card into my pocket, beginning to understand. Quietly Davis takes my hand and walks me through the open gate into the graveyard. Sarah Beth, Jimmy, my father and Cynthia follow. The snow silences our footfalls, it is soft and gentle under our feet. Some graves have evergreen grave blankets and others are decorated with poinsettias and red bows. I am grateful to have the white roses to leave as a token. I walk toward my family's plot, holding Davis's hand. Sometimes not knowing what is coming is easier, and I've learned to trust in Davis and his love for me. I can hear Sarah Beth weeping quietly behind me, and turn to watch as Cynthia gently strokes my father's arm, cradling her own arm in the crook of his elbow.

Davis leads me to a spot I have visited only once, holding both my hands as we wait for my family to gather around us. I avoid his gaze, and the gaze of the others. I don't look down at my mother's grave, either. I lift my face up toward the heavens, letting the snowflakes kiss my cheeks and nose and eyes.

"Tessa, look," Davis gently prods me.

With my father standing by my side, and the man I will love thru my life on the other, I finally look down at my mother's grave. Defined finally, as she would have wanted all along.

CAROLINE CONTESSA WALLACE

1972-1989

LOVING DAUGHTER

LOVING MOTHER

My eyes fill with tears of gratitude for Davis, for my father, and for Henry and Marian. Mostly I weep with gratitude for my mother. The woman who gave me life, who did the best she could. I have made peace with her story and have realized it is a part of mine. I pull out a single rose and place it across the snow, I turn and place one on both Henry and Marian's graves as well. I kiss Davis gently.

I've made my last turn home.

Acknowledgements

Life has a funny way of twisting us around and turning us about. Out of all the mess, there is always light. On the advice of a woman I admire and the love of my people I have learned over the last year that the light gets brighter when you create some for yourself. I also learned that creating light for yourself takes some help. And I have a lot.

Thank you to Susie Poole Anderson at Poole Publishing Services for the "easy" editing and beautiful cover. You made a very nerve-wracking process a breeze and I so appreciate that. Thank you xo

Thank you to Mo Parisian. Without you, there's no book.

Thank you to Tamara Stout, Stacy Walston and Kira Quick for being readers of a very rough third (or was it fourth?) draft and giving me valuable, honest input to help round out Tess's story.

I am blessed with the best family a girl could ask for, both the one I was born into and the one I was blessed enough to marry into. Cliche, I know. But it's true.

One of the things my momma taught me was to surround myself with strong, intelligent, gritty women. I learned well. You know who you are. xo

My E. You challenge me to be better. You are my best friend and the love of my life. Wouldn't want to do life without you.

Coop, Jacko & As... everything I do is because of you. You help me to think outside my box, to see things differently and to not take myself so seriously — I'm still working on this one. Thanks for caring about this book. Thanks for being proud of me. Both of those are gifts I didn't know I needed. Momma loves you. xo

About the Author

Along with using words to make sense of her boy-crazy world on her blog, Confessions of a Daughterless Mother, Lara works as a registered nurse as part of a care management team taking care of elderly patients. She is a former teacher and figure skating coach who loves to walk with her husband and Labrador Lulu, read, write, go to the beach and travel. She is Momma to three boys and has been happily married for nearly twenty-two years. *Last Turn Home* is her first novel.

You can find her at laraalspaugh.com.

71932616R00135

Made in the USA
Middletown, DE
01 May 2018